Ma

2021

THE
FIELD NOTES
OF
Gwen Bell :

BOOTS
and
BUCKETS

THE FIELD NOTES OF GWEN BELL

Summer Ruins

Boots and Buckets

THE FIELD NOTES OF
Gwen Bell:

BOOTS
and
BUCKETS

by

DEB WATLEY

Illustrated by Tiffany Harris

deb watley books

Harrisburg, South Dakota

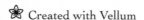 Created with Vellum

To my parents who encouraged me to keep my nose in a book

CHAPTER ONE

Gwen's first day of marching band camp at her new middle school on the first Monday of August was chaos.

The director ran back and forth trying to keep the students lined up in straight rows and columns. "One, two, three, four," he shouted.

Gwen concentrated on the feet of the boy in front of her. "Left, right, left, right," she whispered. But her hiking boots marched right, left, right, left.

Why was this so hard? Although the students were carrying their instruments, they weren't playing any music. All they had to do was stay in line and keep their steps in sync.

She glanced at the other band members lined up on either side of her. They made the squiggliest line of people she'd ever seen, but at least their feet moved in step together. Why wouldn't hers?

She swiveled her head to see the band students behind her.

One girl, carrying cymbals and wearing cowboy boots, marched by herself. The band director waved for some of the other percussionists to get in line next to Boot Girl. They ignored him.

Gwen checked her own feet again. She should've worn sneakers like *most* of the other girls. But since the director had warned them ahead of time to wear comfortable, closed-toe footwear, she had decided to wear the hiking boots she'd worn earlier in the summer. Bad choice. The boots made her feet even hotter now than they'd been a few weeks ago.

She shook her head. Why would someone choose to wear cowboy boots to march? Maybe Boot Girl was as clueless about marching band as she was.

Gwen peeked at the percussion section again.

Boot Girl still marched by herself. It was like she had an invisible bubble between her and everyone else. She noticed Gwen and smiled.

Gwen returned the smile. Maybe this cowgirl would be a new friend.

Suddenly Gwen crashed into the boy in front of her, bumping her knuckles and flute into his back.

"Ow! Back up!"

Gwen looked into his scowl and felt her own face go hot.

"Sorry." She stepped back into her assigned row. That boy was kind of cute, and now she'd never be able to talk to him again. She tipped her head to hide her face behind the brim of her hat. If only she could hide the rest of herself.

The hat did help her avoid the late morning sunshine, but it didn't protect her from the heat and humidity that radiated off the ground and made the air thick and oppressive.

Gwen shook her head to loosen the strands of hair stuck to the back of her sweaty neck. Just then a light breeze lifted her damp strands but also sent a strong odor past her nose.

It wasn't the fragrance of fresh-cut hay fields she'd smelled near the archeology dig where she had spent most of June and July. No. This smell reeked.

It wasn't the acrid smoke from the campfire, nor the dank earth in the dig units, nor even the rank body odor from dirt-covered archeologists. It was worse.

Horse.

The wind cooled the back of her neck again. Gwen got another whiff of horse. She wrinkled her

3

nose and looked behind her to locate the source of the odor.

Gwen sighed.

The smell came from the direction of Boot Girl.

—

After practice Gwen put her flute in its case and guzzled from her water bottle. She stood at the edge of the school yard and watched the other girls talking and putting away their instruments.

She hadn't planned to be by herself, but somehow she was. She looked around and wondered who she should talk to. Her best friend, Olivia, wasn't in band. The other girls were bunched in small groups making afternoon plans with each other. The girls glanced at one another, but no one switched groups.

Gwen looked at the groups and twisted her bracelet. After being away from town for a couple months, even the girls she had known most of her life suddenly seemed like strangers to her. This must be what it felt like to be a new girl.

Her mom had encouraged her to put herself out there during the first day or two at band camp because it was easier to make introductions before people had grouped up. It was already too late.

Maybe it would be easier to talk to someone who was alone.

Gwen sipped her water while she looked around.

Boot Girl sat near the road with her back against a tree trunk, reading a book.

This girl wasn't dressed like the girls Gwen and Olivia usually hung out with. In addition to the cowboy boots, she wore dusty, patched jeans and a t-shirt with a tractor company logo on it. She must live on a farm. Some of the other girls lived on farms, but they were dressed more like Gwen, in shorts and trendy t-shirts.

It probably wasn't Boot Girl's clothes that kept people away from her. It was her horse smell.

Hardly anyone had talked to Gwen today either. Even the girls she knew from her old school seemed to be avoiding her.

Did she smell too? Gwen wiped the sweat off the back of her neck and then took a sneaky sniff of her hand. She didn't notice anything overpowering. Then again, maybe she was just used to her own stink.

Gwen started to walk toward the other girls, but she stopped and twisted her bracelet again. It was unusual for the girls not to include her in their groups. She could just join in, but what if they ignored her? Or worse?

She turned around and looked at Boot Girl again.

She seemed relaxed—even happy.

Gwen remembered her friend Di, one of the college students she'd met at the dig. Di always seemed comfortable with herself, and she was friendly to others. In fact, Di had introduced herself to Gwen. If Di could introduce herself to someone new, then Gwen could too.

Taking a deep breath, Gwen walked over to Boot Girl.

"Hi, I'm Gwen Bell." She plopped on the grass next to the girl. "Ahhh. It feels good to sit. I didn't know we'd march so much on the first day."

"I'm Harper Miller," the girl said. "Yeah, that was hardcore, especially after practicing polo drills with Boots before I came here."

"Boots? Polo?" Gwen wrinkled her brow.

"Polo's like field hockey, except we ride horses," Harper said.

"We have polo in South Dakota?"

"Sure! It's all over the world."

"I thought that was only in England. You know, like the royal family."

"My family's not royalty." Harper shook her head. "But we've been playing polo for years, and our team won a regional championship last year. Boots is my pony."

"So you're good?"

Harper shrugged. "For my age. Where's your farm?"

"I don't live on a farm." Gwen plucked at the grass touching her bare legs. Then it dawned on her that her hiking boots suggested otherwise. "Oh. I wore my boots at my parents' archeology dig. I thought they'd be comfortable for marching. I was wrong."

"Archeologists?" Harper said. "Like in movies when they dig up treasure?"

"Sort of, but not really."

Harper looked confused.

"The only treasures we found were some arrow points and broken dishes." Gwen changed the subject. "Where do you live?"

"A couple miles that way." Harper pointed to the right.

"I live a few blocks from here," Gwen said. "We should've been at the same elementary school. Did you just move to town?"

"Nope. My family has lived here since the late 1800s."

"Why haven't we ever met before?"

"My mom used to work at the other elementary school, so we go—went—to school there."

"We?"

"Yeah, me and my younger sisters and brother."

"How are the cymbals?"

7

"Meh. What else could I play for my first instrument? All I have to do is count."

"You've never played a band instrument?"

"Nope." Harper shrugged again. "My mom made me choose a school activity so I'd make friends."

"I love playing my flute, but I'm not sure about marching band. I didn't know I was such a klutz." Just then Gwen noticed Olivia walking up the sidewalk.

Olivia wore a sundress, strappy sandals, and a bracelet that matched the one Gwen wore. Gwen waved, and Olivia walked over.

"I thought I'd walk you home." Olivia smiled. "Then at least I can see you sometime before school starts."

"Olivia, this is Harper." Gwen stood up. "Harper went to the other elementary school, but she lives close to our neighborhood."

"Whew!" Olivia waved a hand in front of her nose and swiveled. "Something smells. What died?"

Gwen glanced at Harper, expecting to see embarrassment.

Instead, Harper stood and smirked down at Gwen and Olivia. She sniffed in their direction. "The only thing that stinks around here is some flowery perfume."

Just then a white pickup covered in gray dust pulled up to the curb.

"Later, haters," Harper said in a hard voice. She grabbed her book and water bottle and climbed into the passenger seat, and the truck pulled away.

"Well!" Olivia huffed. "I hope I don't have classes with her. Talk about rude."

"You said she smelled." Gwen crossed her arms in front of her chest.

"Did not. I said *something* smelled." Olivia widened her eyes. "Oh, was that her? I thought it was your clothes. And I was joking. Besides, if she's that rude, I just saved you." She studied Gwen's outfit and squinted. "Is that the same outfit you've worn all summer?"

"Uh," Gwen said. "Sort of."

"Let's go window-shopping this afternoon!"

"I'm helping Mom put away artifacts, remember? I can go tomorrow." Gwen grabbed her flute case, and the girls started walking down the street toward their houses.

"Can't. Don't *you* remember?" Olivia narrowed her eyes. "My family's going to Omaha for the rest of the week."

"Then why do you want to go shopping today?" Gwen said.

"Who needs a reason? Who are you?" Olivia

demanded, putting her hands on her hips. "Last year by this time we'd already planned our first week of outfits."

"I've been busy."

Olivia grunted. "No kidding. The archeology dig, vacation, artifacts, Clay, Cooper, Di, blah, blah, blah. I've been waiting all summer to go window-shopping with you."

Gwen laughed. "Exaggerate much?"

"Am I?" Olivia pointed at Gwen's outfit and frowned. "You need to get some new clothes. Those are shabby. Don't even get me started on your hiking boots. First impressions are important. Girls can act mean to others who don't look like everybody else."

"Like you just did to Harper?"

"I told you, I was talking about you." Olivia flipped her hair.

"Well, I don't want friends who only like me for what I look like," Gwen said, fanning herself with her hat. She was surprised at how little she cared about her school clothes anymore. "That's so immature."

"Maybe I'm not mature enough to hang out with you."

"That's not what I meant." Gwen twisted her bracelet. "I just wish we could talk about other stuff sometimes."

Olivia glared at her. "Talking about fashion used

to be our thing. Now it's all Di and the dig. You haven't even asked me what I did all summer! You could be a better friend." Olivia turned at her street corner and started toward her house. She turned back to Gwen. "I'll see if Erin wants to go with me. Enjoy your artifacts."

Gwen called after her, "Erin who?"

FIELD NOTES

CHAPTER TWO

That evening, Gwen sat on the rug in her room, opened her laptop, and video called Di.

When Di answered and turned on her video and audio, Gwen started talking. "I just had a rotten day."

"What happened?"

Gwen counted on her fingers. "Fight with Olivia. Band camp, but can't march. Tried to be nice to newish girl, but she ended up being rude."

"Rough day! Tomorrow will be better."

"I hope so." Gwen sighed.

"Listen," Di said, leaning into the screen. "I've got some exciting news!"

"You're going to switch to my mom and dad's university?"

"I'd love to have classes with them, but that's not

it." Di paused and took a breath. "I'm joining the Army."

Gwen wondered if she'd heard correctly. "What?"

"I'm joining the Army. I leave for Basic Training in September."

Gwen felt her face fall, but then remembered Di could see her on her computer screen. She shook herself. "What about school?"

"I'll get my education through the military. Just think of it as me changing schools."

"But you might have to go to war!" Gwen said, picturing Di in combat gear in some kind of shootout.

"Maybe." Di shrugged. "That's part of the deal."

Gwen's throat tightened so much she barely croaked out, "Why?"

"I wanted to last year. Serving our country is a big deal in my family. I want to do my part. My dad asked me to go to college for a year. He wanted me to experience another option and to think it through before I decided. I did that. I still want to enlist."

"What if you're killed?" Gwen wished she could take back her words, but suddenly she couldn't breathe.

"That could happen, but it's not likely. I could die here too. I don't want to live my life in fear of bad stuff." Di paused. "However, I won't be home much for the next four years."

Gwen swallowed and tried not to cry. With Olivia mad at her, and the other girls avoiding her, Di might be her only real friend. And now Gwen wouldn't see her for four years—and maybe never.

"Gwen," Di said, "I've got more news."

Gwen wiped away the tear that was running down her cheek. She couldn't get her voice to work so she just nodded.

"My family and a few of my friends are going to do a week-long trail ride and camping trip in Colorado in September," Di said. "I'm inviting you too!"

"Yes!" Gwen bobbed her head. Then she bit her lip. "Wait. Camping. Does that mean tents and hiking and cooking over a fire?"

Di nodded. "Mostly. There are places we won't be able to have a fire because of wildfire danger."

Gwen realized that after surviving half the summer at her parents' dig, surely she could handle roughing it for a week in the woods. It would be worth it if she could see Di one last time. Besides, riding an ATV sounded like fun.

"I'll have to ask my parents. But we don't have a four-wheeler."

"A four-wheeler?" Di furrowed her brow. "I didn't say anything about four-wheelers."

"You said trail ride."

"Not on ATVs." Di laughed. "On horseback."

Horses! Gwen sat back in her chair. Why did it have to be horses? They were fast, huge, strong, and stinky . . . and she had no idea how to ride one.

"Does that make a difference to you?"

"We don't have one of those, either," Gwen said.

"No problem, we're going to a ranch that is providing the horses and a guide for our trip."

"I hope I can come." Gwen wasn't about to admit that she was afraid of horses and had never ridden one.

"I hope you can come too. I've told my family all about you, and they'd love to meet you. It's only a month away."

Gwen nodded as she said goodbye to Di. This could be her last chance to see her friend. How would she learn to ride well enough in just four weeks? How would she overcome her fear to even get on a horse?

Gwen walked into the living room to talk with her mom who was sitting on the sofa typing on her laptop. Gwen plopped down on the floor next to her.

"Thanks for your help this afternoon," her mom said. "Now I can finish my field school report, plan my classes, and then help you get ready for the first day of school."

Gwen let out a big sigh.

"What's wrong?" Her mom stroked Gwen's hair.

"Di is joining the Army."

"Good for her. I'm not surprised."

"Really?"

"She's very focused. She's going to excel in the military."

"But she's my friend, and she's going to be gone for four years. What if she gets killed?"

"I'm sure she's thought through the risks." Her mom wrapped an arm around Gwen. "You know, soldiers get breaks during their enlistments and they usually have Internet access. You two will be able to stay in contact."

She brushed a strand of hair out of Gwen's face. "Besides, you and Olivia will have so much fun over the next four years that the time will seem to fly by."

"Olivia doesn't get me anymore." Gwen frowned. "All she cares about is shopping and clothes."

"And you have other interests?"

"Yeah." Gwen turned around to face her mom. "I could see Di again before she goes off to training. She invited me to her family's camping trip in Colorado next month. It's for a week."

"How lovely! I'll check about getting school excused for you. I know you'd be able to work ahead or catch up on work you've missed. And often the best education comes outside the classroom."

"I've never heard a teacher say that before."

"A big part of my teaching happens at field school," her mom said, "not in a classroom."

"There's a problem." Gwen twisted the end of her ponytail. "It's a trail ride. With horses."

"I don't think you've ever ridden a horse."

Gwen shook her head.

"A week-long trail ride doesn't sound like a ride for a beginner."

"I want to go," Gwen said, ignoring her fear. Little kids rode horses. Surely she could do it too. "Please? This might be my last time to ever see Di."

"I need more details, of course," her mom said. "But your lack of horse experience bothers me. I'll talk to Di. Meanwhile, you research places nearby that give lessons and what they would cost."

"I will." Gwen nodded.

"Don't get your hopes up," her mom said. "A month to learn how to ride a horse well enough for a camping trip sounds unrealistic."

FIELD NOTES

CHAPTER THREE

Tuesday morning before the band camp session began, Gwen approached the group of sixth grade girls sitting on benches in front of the school.

She had taken Olivia's advice and dressed in a white tank top that had pink polka-dots, solid pink shorts, and sneakers. She had a distinct tan line on her calves from wearing socks and hiking boots all summer, but her feet felt light and cool.

Gwen lifted her chin and stood up straighter. She looked just like the other girls.

One girl scooted over to make room for Gwen to sit. The girls were laughing and talking with each other, and Gwen learned the names of the girls she hadn't met before.

She leaned back and blew a hair out of her face. It

was nice to be in a group of girls again. She looked at "Harper's tree" where Harper was reading a book.

Harper and Gwen had been having a good conversation yesterday before Olivia joined them. Maybe Harper and Gwen liked similar things. Maybe she could teach Gwen a little about horses. Maybe Harper wanted to join the other girls but felt too shy —like Gwen had felt yesterday.

But Harper had been unkind to Gwen and Olivia. Only because she thought Olivia had insulted her, Gwen admitted to herself. Harper probably felt hurt.

When Harper looked up, Gwen waved to her and motioned for her to join the group.

Harper raised her book in front of her face.

How rude! Gwen's face burned. Didn't Harper want others to be nice to her?

"Don't let her bother you," the girl next to Gwen said. "She went to my elementary school and has always been stuck-up. If you can get her to talk, all she wants to talk about is horses. We've quit trying. She thinks she's a cowgirl or something."

As the other girls talked about school starting in two weeks, and about clothes and boys, Gwen's mind wandered, and her eyes kept going back to Harper. Was Harper really stuck-up? Or was she just afraid to join the group? Or did she like being by herself?

Maybe Harper was like Di and did what she liked, even if she did it by herself.

Gwen wasn't sure she could be that brave.

—

That afternoon Gwen sat on her bed watching videos of marching bands on her laptop. She sighed and pushed her laptop to the side.

Some bands had performed complicated field shows where the musicians marched all over the football field. How did they know where they were supposed to be? She was still trying to march in a straight line and stay in step with the people around her.

She texted Olivia.

"How's the trip?"

"Nothing special yet. Mom says I have to put my phone away for the rest of the vacation. Talk to you next week. We'll do our school shopping."

Gwen rolled her eyes and put her phone away.

Even when Olivia got back, she only wanted to talk clothes. Gwen wanted to talk about band, the arrow points she'd found at the dig, and Clay and Cooper, the little boys she'd babysat. What were they doing now? Riding their bikes? Did they miss her?

Did Di miss her? Probably not. The boys had each other, and Di had her own family and friends.

Gwen only had her mom and dad, but they were at the university preparing for their fall classes. At least this year her mom was going back to teaching part-time again and would be home more often.

The house was quiet. Gwen wandered from room to room, ending up in the living room. She turned on the TV. The sound of the voices helped make the house seem less empty.

Olivia's laughter was usually good at keeping things from being too quiet, but they weren't really on the same page anymore. Even the other girls from school were stuck on clothes and boys. Gwen was so beyond that.

Di was the only one who seemed to understand her. It wouldn't be so bad to be friendless at school if she could talk with Di often. But that wasn't going to be possible now for a long time.

Gwen just *had* to go on the trail ride.

She opened her laptop to look up information about riding lessons. A couple stables in the Yankton area offered lessons but they seemed expensive. She hated to ask her parents for the money.

She had planned to use her summer babysitting money to buy clothes for school. But she wouldn't have enough money to pay for clothes and lessons. If only she had a friend who could teach her how to ride for free.

Harper?

Gwen shook her head. They weren't friends. In fact, Harper had refused to even sit with Gwen at band camp, so why would she help Gwen?

Gwen could pay her a little. Or do some kind of trade. Did she have any skills? She could help Harper make friends with her sixth-grade friends. But how? Gwen knew a little about clothes. Maybe she could teach Harper how to dress like the others.

But what if the other girls still excluded Harper? Would they end up rejecting Gwen too? What would Olivia do?

Yet if Gwen didn't try, she wouldn't see Di for years, and maybe never.

As Gwen sorted through her thoughts, she gazed at the TV without really seeing it. Finally she noticed it was broadcasting a show about the end of World War II. Gwen stared at the images of soldiers crawling up a beach. She shivered and turned off the TV.

Yes, she would see Di.

If Gwen was careful, she could keep any fashion and riding lessons with Harper a secret for a few weeks.

Now she just had to convince Harper to help her.

FIELD NOTES

AUGUST

Sun	Mon	Tues	Wed	Thu	Fri	Sat
2	3 1st day of BAND CAMP!	4	5	6	7	8
9	10	11	12	13	14	15
16	17	18	19 1st day of School	20 60°	21	22
23	24	25	26	27	28	29

→ BAND CAMP ♫

← BAND CAMP some more! ♫

SEPTEMBER

Sun	Mon	Tues	Wed	Thu	Fri	Sat
30	31	1	2	3	4	5
6	7 Yechaw!	8 Yippee!	9	10	11	12
13	14	15	16	17	18	19
20	21	22	23	24	25 oops!	26 27, 28 29, 30

TRAIL Ride with Di →

CHAPTER FOUR

Gwen arrived at band camp early Wednesday morning and waited in the shade of Harper's tree. She looked around at the empty school yard. If Harper arrived soon, Gwen could get this deal made before many others showed up.

Gwen smoothed her shirt and adjusted her ponytail. She checked her painted fingernails and jingled her bracelet.

Soon the dusty white pick-up truck pulled up to the curb.

Harper got out and saw Gwen by the tree, so she changed directions and headed toward the side school yard where the band would practice.

Gwen grabbed her flute case from the grass and approached Harper. "Hi, Harper—" Gwen made her voice as friendly as she could.

"No boots today?" Harper said. "Or your really nice friend?"

Gwen shook her head. "Um, no." She paused. "Sorry about Olivia. She was trying to tease me."

"Right."

"Seriously. Olivia had been on me to quit wearing my dig clothes."

"She succeeded," Harper said. "Those fingernails and shorts don't scream 'let's go digging.'"

Walking backward in front of Harper, Gwen motioned with her free hand toward herself. "This is normally how I dress."

"So you're one of those girls who thinks clothes are the most important thing in the world." Harper made it a statement, not a question.

Gwen felt a tremor of anger. This wasn't going the direction she intended.

"No. But I like bright colors, and I like to mix and match my clothes and make different outfits. I think it's fun."

"That's boring. Fun is scoring during the last chukker of a match."

"I have no clue what you just said." Gwen stopped and put out her hand to keep Harper from walking past her. "Listen, I have an idea that could help both of us."

"This ought to be good." Harper crossed her arms and looked down at Gwen.

"I am good at putting outfits together. If you wanted, I could give you some clothing tips. Just tweaks. Not to change your style . . . just to freshen it up."

"Why would I want help with my clothes?" Harper narrowed her eyes. "Are you judging me? Am I not good enough to be in your presence, Your Majesty?"

"No. Yes." Gwen started to shake her head and then frowned. "That's not how I meant it. But if you dressed like the other girls, you'd fit in better." Gwen bit her lip. She hadn't meant to say that. She sounded as harsh as Olivia had the other day when she told Gwen that she needed to dress better so she could make friends.

Gwen twisted her bracelet and thought through how to say her next words. "Even celebrities who love fashion have stylists to keep them trendy. I could be your personal stylist."

"Why are you so desperate to save me from fashion ignorance?"

"I want help too. Riding lessons. I have a chance to go on a camping trip with horses, but I don't know anything about horses." Gwen paused. She had gone this far, she might as well take the rest of the plunge. "Actually, I'm scared of them."

She held her breath as she waited for Harper's response. Not only would Harper probably say no, but Gwen had just given her some more ammo to make fun of her.

"I like my clothes and my style," Harper said.

Gwen thought quickly through her other options. "I could help you with homework. Or I could pay $100."

Harper gazed into the distance for a long minute.

Gwen picked at the polish on her fingernails while she waited. "Thanks, anyway." Gwen turned to go, looking for a place she could hide for a while.

"Hey," Harper said. "You know about archeology, right?"

"A little." Gwen shrugged.

"I'll teach you how to ride, if you help me find something at my farm."

"Find what?"

Harper looked around and then leaned closer to Gwen. "A treasure."

Gwen rolled her eyes. "I told you. Real archeology isn't like that."

"Sometimes it is," Harper said. "Last night I watched a TV show about archeologists who found an old pirate ship loaded with gold."

"Do you think there's some old pirate ship buried on your farm?"

"Of course not," Harper said, raising her voice. "I'm not stupid." Then she whispered, "But I think there is a treasure somewhere on the farm."

"What?" Now Gwen was curious.

"We think that Basil Miller, my great-great-great-great-grandfather, hid some gold on our land. Maybe he mined at a gold rush, or maybe he got some in a nefarious way and then hid it."

"Nefarious?" Gwen asked.

"Illegal . . . unethical," Harper said. "Read more books."

Gwen wondered if learning to ride a horse and seeing Di was worth this. But she leaned forward. "Just go on."

"Our family legend is that Basil said he had a fortune but never told his family where or what it was."

"They probably spent it," Gwen said, frowning.

"I don't think so." Harper shook her head. "Because my ancestors have searched for it for years and years. Even my dad looked for it when he was young. Why would everyone keep looking for it if it was already found or spent?"

"Your farm is probably huge! It would take forever!"

Harper brushed off Gwen's warning. "You could help me narrow it down. I know we might not find it. But we might. I gotta try."

"Why?"

"Never mind. Deal?"

Gwen twisted her bracelet. This wasn't the deal she wanted or expected, but it would help her get to the trail ride. She nodded to Harper. "Deal."

"Come out to my house after band camp tomorrow." Harper pulled out her phone. "Let's trade numbers."

The girls tapped their numbers into each other's phones. Gwen had thought her hand-me-down phone from her mom was old, but Harper's was even older.

When Gwen put her own phone back into her pocket, the reality of their deal sank in, and she gulped.

Tomorrow she'd have to ride a horse *and* look for a treasure that probably didn't exist. She didn't know which one was more impossible.

FIELD NOTES

CHAPTER FIVE

That night after supper, Gwen's dad went to the other room to work on his book, and Gwen cleared the table while her mom sat and sipped her lemonade.

"Mom, when we were at the field school dig, how would you have known where to dig if you didn't have Dr. Sanchez's geophysics equipment?"

"We would've taken some core samples."

"What's that?"

"We'd push a metal cylinder into the ground. When we pull it back up, we'd have a cylinder of soil where we could see how the soil changed from layer to layer. We can do a lot of core samples quickly to narrow down where we want to put a dig unit."

Gwen scraped and stacked the plates on the counter. Core samples and soil layers sounded complicated. "What would you do if you couldn't do a core sample?"

"Field surveys," her mom said. "We'd just walk over an area and see what we could see. Like an eroded hillside that shows the soil layers or even artifacts. Sometimes we might see the remains of a building foundation or depressions in the ground where a lodge had been located or where something might have been buried."

"Oh," Gwen said. Starting Harper's treasure hunt/dig was sounding more and more complicated.

"Why do you ask?"

"I'm going to help someone with a treasure hunt."

Gwen's mom raised an eyebrow. "Tell me more."

"There's this girl at band camp—Harper—who wants me to help her find a buried treasure on her farm."

"Why does she want your help?"

"It's payment."

"What do you mean?"

"I'm going to help her look for the treasure, and she's going to teach me how to ride a horse."

"What?" Her mom sat up straight.

Before she could say, "No way," Gwen hurriedly explained the reasoning behind the deal. "I looked up prices for lessons, and they're expensive. Harper is an expert. She even plays polo, and her family's team won some kind of championship, so her parents must be experts too."

Gwen's mom rubbed her forehead. "I'm not sure about this deal."

"Please? I want to go with Di on her trail ride, and this seems like my best option."

"But is it a safe option? Let me talk to Harper's parents first."

Gwen gave her mom Harper's contact info. Then she washed the dishes while her mom took her phone to her bedroom so she could talk with Harpers' mom privately.

When she returned to the kitchen, Gwen turned around, dripping water on the floor. "What's the verdict?"

"We'll give it a try. Mrs. Miller said Harper and her siblings have been riding their whole lives. She knows her horses and will be careful. But you have to promise me you'll wear one of their helmets."

"Thank you!" Gwen bounced on her feet. "Did you tell them about the treasure hunt?"

"Yes. Mrs. Miller said you may look as much as you want." Then Gwen's mom held out her hand. "But you *must* get permission before you do any digging so Harper's parents can make sure there aren't any buried wires or pipes."

Gwen hugged her mom.

"Ooh, you're wet." Her mom laughed and guided Gwen back to the sink. "What do you know about this treasure?"

"Harper thinks her great-great-something-grand-father buried gold somewhere on their farm."

"If you find it, I want to know all about it. That would be very interesting local history." Her mom poured herself another glass of lemonade and sat at the table.

"I don't think we'll find anything."

"You never know. Family stories that get passed on from generation to generation often get exaggerated or turn out to be totally wrong. But sometimes they lead to . . . pure gold."

"Mom." Gwen rolled her eyes. "That was a bad pun. If there really is gold, how would we find it? I don't even know where to start."

"Start at the beginning." Her mother grinned.

"Mom!"

"Seriously. Find out as much as you can about Harper's ancestor, their land during his time, and more about the family story. There might be diaries or photographs. The courthouse would have some land records. Read old newspaper articles and obituaries."

Gwen noticed the excitement in her mother's voice. Her mom loved how archeologists were like detectives looking for clues and trying to solve old mysteries. Gwen also remembered when she, personally, had read articles and books from the library when she was trying to research the area where she did her secret dig.

"Old newspapers are a treasure in themselves," her mom continued. "They're full of all kinds of juicy details that modern papers don't have. Diaries and newspaper articles are primary resources from people who were witnesses. Sometimes they're wrong, though, so you have to double-check the facts with other sources."

Gwen nodded. "Tomorrow afternoon I'm supposed to go to Harper's house after band camp."

"I can be home for lunch tomorrow and then drop you off at Harper's on my way back to work." Her mom tapped her finger to her lips. "I was just thinking you could use your dad's metal detector."

"We didn't use them at the field school."

"No, but they can be helpful. Say we're surveying an old battlefield. The detectors can locate old musket balls, buttons from uniforms, things like that. If it detected something, you shouldn't have to dig more than a few inches. It might be a help."

"I don't know how to use a detector."

"C'mon, I'll show you how it works, and then I'll show you how to do laundry. You can deal with your horsey-smelling clothes yourself."

Gwen groaned and followed her mom to the garage. It wasn't like treasure hunting and riding lessons were her only projects at the moment. She also had to figure out how to march and to memorize two songs for band. The director had announced that assignment at band camp that morning.

Fortunately, one was *The Star-Spangled Banner*. Gwen had already memorized a slightly different arrangement during the summer, so the one for band wouldn't be difficult to master.

It was also a good thing Olivia was out of town for a few days. Gwen didn't need Olivia to know about the time she was spending with Harper or to distract her from band and horse riding. But the archeology part of her bargain with Harper was going to be a huge distraction.

FIELD NOTES

CHAPTER SIX

On Thursday afternoon, Harper met Gwen at the gravel driveway of her family's farm as Gwen exited the car.

"Hi, I'm Dr. Bell," Gwen's mom said through her open window. "Is your mom around? I thought I'd introduce myself."

Harper shook her head. "She's getting a part for the tractor. She took my sisters and brother with her. They'll be back soon."

"Then I'll say hi when I pick up Gwen. Have fun!" She waved and pulled out of the drive.

"What are you wearing?" Harper said, pointing at Gwen.

Gwen looked down at her shirt and shorts. "These are old clothes that are okay for getting dirty and stinky."

"You're going to regret wearing shorts," Harper said.

"Why?" Gwen studied Harper's outfit: a t-shirt, jeans, ball cap, and cowboy boots. "Aren't you roasting? It's ninety degrees today! Ouch!" She swatted the big horsefly that just bit her leg.

Harper laughed. "That's why. There are always biting flies. And your thighs are going to get all chafed from the saddle."

"Why didn't you tell me that this morning?"

"I thought you'd know," Harper said. "Your shoes, however, are the big problem."

Gwen looked at her shoes.

"These are my oldest sneakers, in case I step in any horse poo. Then I can throw them away after the trail ride. I thought I was being practical."

"You need boots."

"Why?" Gwen sighed. Apparently boots were now a permanent part of her life.

"The heel on the boots keep your feet in the stirrups. Without a heel your foot could go all the way through, and you could get caught in it and dragged by your ankle if you fell off."

Fall off? Dragged by a horse? Gwen shuddered. Riding sounded more and more dangerous. "My hiking boots have a heel. Would they work?"

"Maybe." Harper led Gwen down the drive to the

open garage attached to a white two-story farmhouse. A covered porch wrapped around the front to the far side of the house, and a dog slept in the shade of the porch. "Why didn't you bring them today? I thought you wore boots for digging."

"Because we're not digging today. We're going to plan out our search."

Harper put her hands on her hips and scowled. "We don't have much summer left, you know. Bring your boots next time so you can try them, but the bulky soles might keep you from feeling the stirrups." Harper motioned Gwen into the garage. "Today you can wear an old pair of mine. We should have something that works."

Gwen's jaw dropped. Shelves lined one wall of the garage and were filled with a variety of well-worn cowboy boots, tall black boots, mud boots, and even snow boots.

"You could open a boot store!"

"We don't throw them away when we outgrow them because another sibling or a visitor always needs a pair."

Gwen tried on several cowboy boots and found a pair that fit tight but didn't pinch her toes. Would she have to wear spurs too? She imagined herself walking with spurs on the boots and laughed as she pictured herself jangling with each step.

"What's so funny?"

"Nothing," Gwen said, shaking her head. "Just trying to get used to the boots."

"What's to get used to? They're comfortable and practical."

"You've probably been wearing them since you could walk."

"Before. I had baby boots that my mom uses for Christmas tree ornaments now. Come on, you can meet my Boots." Harper walked around the house.

Gwen followed. "Very punny."

Harper's house sat near the gravel road at the top of a hill and was partially hidden from the road by dark green spruce trees. A few loaded apple trees and a garden grew on the far side of the house.

Near the garage, the driveway split off and went a short way down the hill past a barn, a tractor, and a line of huge round bales of hay.

Gwen stopped and looked around. Behind the house was a large yard with towering shade trees, a kids' wading pool, and an old-fashioned-looking play-house. A few chickens wandered around the yard, pecking at insects. A breeze rustled the leaves in the trees, and somewhere down the hill a horse neighed.

"Quit dawdling," Harper called over her shoulder.

Gwen hurried to catch up with Harper halfway down the hill, almost to the stable and some big fenced-in areas. One was grassy, probably a pasture. The other was mostly dirt. The wind kicked up little swirls of dust and carried odors of manure. Gwen wrinkled her nose.

Harper led Gwen to a wood rail fence by the pasture just as a huge horse came up to Harper from the other side.

The dark reddish-brown horse had a white spot on its nose, a black tail, and white from its back hooves almost halfway up its legs.

"Gwen, this is Boots."

Gwen looked up—and up—at the horse.

"I thought you said Boots was a pony," Gwen said, catching her breath and backing several steps away from the horse. Was she going to have to ride that giant?

"She's my polo pony." Harper reached over the fence and patted the side of Boots' neck. "That's what horses in polo are called. But she's a full-size horse."

Gwen focused on the parts of the horse closer to the ground. "Are her white legs why you call her Boots?"

Harper nodded. "Those markings are really called stockings, but I thought Boots sounded better."

Gwen looked over the horse again. Something wasn't right. "Where's her hair?"

"What do you mean?" Harper narrowed her eyes.

Gwen pointed to the top of the horse's head. "Her hair?"

"Oh, her mane. It gets in the way for polo so we roach it."

"You do what?"

"Roach it." Harper petted the short bits of mane sticking straight up on Boots' neck. "That's the word for cutting it like this."

Gwen touched the end of her own ponytail. She'd never sacrifice her hair for a sport. But she watched as the horse shook her head. Even without a mane, Boots moved gracefully, like a queen who enjoyed being admired by everyone in her presence.

"She's beautiful," Gwen said, barely breathing.

"And smart," Harper said. "And way too much horse for you to ride. I'm going to teach you on Ruby." Harper led the way into the open stable door. "I've already got her in the crossties."

Crossties? When Gwen stepped into the dark stable, her eyes slowly adjusted to the lower light, but her stomach tightened like a hairband stretched too tight. She hoped Ruby wasn't as big as Boots.

FIELD NOTES

CHAPTER SEVEN

"Phew!" A sour stench made Gwen gag. "What is that smell?"

Harper laughed as Gwen pinched her nose.

"Horse, sweat, insect repellent, and manure," Harper said. "It could be worse. The horses don't spend much time in their stalls, and we clean them out all the time when we do use them. You should smell the manure pile behind the barn."

Harper squared her shoulders and lifted her chin. "I'm going to turn you into a real rider, and then you'll be proud to smell like horse."

"You're joking, right?" Gwen said.

Just then a couple kittens chased each other past the girls.

"Oh," Gwen exclaimed, glad to focus on the kittens instead of the odor. "They're so cute!"

Harper bent over and picked up both kittens. She handed one to Gwen and cuddled the other one in her arms, scratching it under the chin. "Their mother disappeared, so I bottle-fed these two. They think I'm their mama."

Gwen copied how Harper scratched the kitten. Harper was so gentle with it. Gwen hadn't seen a kind side of Harper since their first conversation before Olivia messed things up.

The kitten in her own arms stretched its neck, closed its eyes, and purred.

"Aww." Gwen relaxed, too, and the tightness left her stomach. "We could never have pets because my parents travel every summer. They always say, 'It's not fair to board an animal for weeks and weeks.'"

"I couldn't live without my cats, and dog, and Boots," Harper whispered. She looked away, hugged the kitten, and set it back on the ground. "Let's get going."

The girls walked past about eight empty stalls.

"This is a big stable," Gwen said.

"We used to have six horses, but the spring flooding messed up planting, and then summer was so dry that what we have planted isn't doing so great. We have more bills coming this fall. Since we probably won't be able to pay for all their feed this winter, we sold our other four horses."

"Sorry." Gwen understood a little about strained family finances, but her family had never had to sell things that were precious to them.

Harper swallowed and motioned Gwen forward.

The girls walked to the last two stalls. These didn't have doors like the previous ones. A dark reddish-brown horse stood in the last one. Ruby looked a lot like Boots, except she didn't have any white markings, and she did have a long black mane.

A rope was connected to both side walls and also to each side of Ruby's halter, keeping her from moving too much.

"Oh, crossties," Gwen said. "I get it."

Harper stood to the side of the horse and stroked her neck. "Ruby is Boots' mother. She's more easy-going than Boots, and she'll help teach you how to ride."

The horse glanced at Gwen and snorted.

Gwen twisted her shirt tail around a finger. She didn't know if she could do this.

"Come closer," Harper insisted. "Back here by her shoulder so she can see you well."

Gwen took a step closer to the horse, but she kept behind Harper. "Hi, Ruby."

The horse snorted again and shook her head.

Gwen jumped back.

"You really haven't been around horses much, have you?" Harper said.

Gwen's face grew hot. "I told you so!"

"Ruby doesn't know you yet. Put your hand out like this, palm up, under her nose. Let her smell you. Keep your fingers straight."

Gwen stepped forward again and put her hand out, but close to her own body.

"Closer," Harper said in a stern voice.

Gwen stuck her hand a couple inches nearer to Ruby.

Then Harper pulled a piece of carrot out her pocket and put it on Gwen's palm. "Be still and let Ruby come to you. Talk to her, too, so she learns your voice."

Gwen pinched her eyes shut and waited for Ruby to lower her head to Gwen's shaking hand.

"Hi, again, Ruby. I'm Gwen. I've never fed a horse before. Don't bite me, please." Gwen opened one eye.

Ruby sniffed the carrot and blew her hot breath on Gwen's hand. Her whiskers tickled Gwen's palm.

Gwen gasped and curled her fingers around the carrot.

"Keep your palm open!"

Gwen held her breath and slowly relaxed her fingers. Ruby took the carrot from Gwen, again tickling her palm.

Gwen snatched her hand away from the horse and giggled nervously.

"Now pet the side of her face and keep talking to her," Harper ordered.

"Is she always so bossy?" Gwen whispered to the horse as she slowly reached up and stroked the side of Ruby's face. "Wow! Ruby, you are so soft."

"If you think that's soft you should pet her nose, between her nostrils."

Gwen touched Ruby's nose with her fingertips. "Like velvet."

"Keep petting. Work your way all the way up her face, scratch behind her ears and near the roots of her mane. Then pet her neck with long strokes."

Ruby's neck felt like one solid muscle. She was enormous and powerful. She could do whatever she wanted.

How would Gwen ride her?

"I groomed her and picked her hooves before you got here." Harper grabbed a blanket off the side half-wall and tossed it over Ruby's back and did the same with the saddle. "I'll saddle her, so watch carefully so you can do it next time."

"Wait. What's all this stuff called?"

Harper pointed at each item. "Halter, bridle, bit, reins, saddle, blanket, and cinch strap." She reached under Ruby's belly, grabbed the dangling cinch, and fastened it to the D-shaped ring on the side of the saddle. Then she slid the halter off Ruby and eased the bit into the horse's mouth and the bridle over her ears.

"Put this on and tighten the straps." Harper handed Gwen a helmet. Then she took the reins in her right hand and walked Ruby toward an open door.

Gwen followed.

"Get up here! Stay away from her back legs if you don't want to get stepped on or kicked."

Hot-faced again, Gwen hurried to Harper's left side. She glanced back at Ruby's hooves and noticed how big they were — bigger than Gwen's hand.

Ruby could stomp Gwen into the ground if she wanted, but she followed Harper like a puppy.

"How do you get her to follow you?" Gwen asked.

"I'm bossy." Harper smirked.

The girls and the horse walked over to the fence-in area with the dirt-covered ground. Harper called it the arena.

Once inside, Harper turned around and shut the gate. She tightened Ruby's cinch strap, looped the end of the reins over Ruby's neck, and held the reins close to the horse's mouth to keep her still. "Okay, Gwen, get on."

Gwen edged to Ruby's side. The stirrup was higher than her waist, and the saddle was even with her head. So high. She lifted a foot but missed the stirrup. She gulped. "How?"

Harper shook her head. "I'm just messing with you. See that step stool on the other side of the fence? Reach between the rails and grab that."

Harper took it from Gwen and set it next to Ruby.

"Okay. Climb up, grab her mane and the reins with your left hand and the back of the saddle with your right. Put your left foot into the stirrup."

Gwen obeyed.

"Now, hop up!"

Gwen stretched her right leg over Ruby's back and let her rear settle into the saddle. She was up.

"Put your feet in the stirrups."

Gwen leaned over Ruby's side so she could see where to put her feet. She stared at the ground. It was so far away. Her fingers tightened around the saddle horn and she sat straight up, holding her body as stiff as possible so she wouldn't fall. She held her breath.

Harper took each of Gwen's feet and placed them in the stirrups. "Relax. If you ride that stiffly you're going to bounce in the saddle and your rear is going to be super sore."

Harper started to lead Ruby at a walk.

As soon as the horse moved, Gwen opened her eyes, clenched her teeth, and broke out in a sweat. She could feel the horse's power under her.

"Slow down!" Gwen's vision started to get blurry. The ground seemed to sway. Maybe it was Gwen that swayed.

"We can't go any slower," Harper said. "Cowgirl up!"

"What?"

"Be brave!"

Gwen leaned forward gripping Ruby's mane. "Stop!"

"You're not going to fall." Harper stopped walking. She put her hands on her hips as she looked up at Gwen. "You need to trust Ruby."

"I want off! Now!"

"She's not going to hurt you unless you do something stupid."

"But I don't know if I'm doing something stupid."

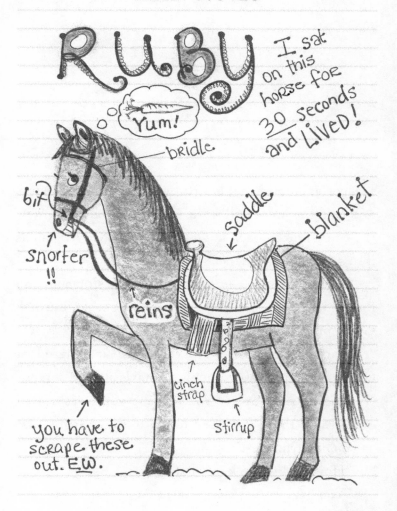

CHAPTER EIGHT

Harper grumbled and led Ruby back to the step stool and held the horse still while Gwen dismounted.

Ruby looked back at Gwen and swished her tail as if to say, "Good riddance."

Gwen crossed her arms over her stomach and forced herself to breathe slowly. Her cheeks burned. Gwen prayed Harper wouldn't tell anyone.

Harper pressed her lips together and stared at Gwen. "We probably shouldn't have started lessons with riding right away. You told me you were scared of horses. I think you need to get to know Ruby first so you can trust her."

"How do I get to know her?"

"You help me with my chores."

"Chores aren't part of our agreement."

"Do you expect to have servants on your trip?"

Harper put a hand on her hip. "You're going to have to know how to take care of a horse. Besides, it's a fast way to get to know them. And if you're nervous every time you're near horses, they'll sense it, and then they might become nervous. If you're calm and confident, they're more likely to be calm."

"What are your chores?"

"We'll groom Ruby and Boots. Water them. Talk to them."

Gwen was breathing a little easier now. "Okay."

"Here, you lead Ruby." Harper handed the reins to Gwen. "Just stay to the left of her head."

Gwen reluctantly took the reins in her right hand. "Like this?"

Harper nodded. "And then hold the dangling part of the reins in your left."

"Okay, Ruby," Gwen said. "Let's go."

As soon as Ruby felt the tug on the reins, she walked next to Gwen.

Back in the stall with the crossties, Harper showed her how to brush Ruby.

"You do it now. I'll put the tack away. Just don't go past Ruby's flank until I'm back. And talk to her."

Gwen nodded and then said, "What's a flank?"

Harper rolled her eyes and pointed to Ruby's side between her ribs and hind hip.

When Harper left her alone, Gwen gulped and

decided to start at the beginning, like she was just meeting Ruby. She felt tiny next to this big animal. Gwen held out her hand, palm up, in front of Ruby's nose and let the horse smell her. She took a deep breath and pretended she was confident.

"Hi, Ruby. I'm Gwen. I'm trying to cowgirl up." Gwen stroked what had to be the softest nose in the world. "I need to see Di. So I have to learn how to ride. But how am I going to be able to ride for days when I can't even make it for two minutes?"

Ruby nodded her head like she was answering Gwen.

Gwen brushed Ruby's neck and shoulder. Her strokes dislodged dust that floated through the air, tickling Gwen's nose.

"Harper said you're going to teach me how to ride. Can you teach me to be brave too?"

As Gwen continued brushing the horse, she felt her own muscles relax and her breathing slowed. There was something mesmerizing about concentrating on her brush strokes. Maybe, just maybe, she could get used to horses.

When Harper came back, she finished brushing Ruby and showed Gwen how to pick the horse's hooves. "They're pretty clean already because I did this earlier. It's really important to make sure we get all the rocks, dirt, and manure out. It can really hurt a horse to walk on a rock, and their feet stay healthier if we keep them clean."

Harper and Gwen took Ruby to the pasture and released her next to Boots. Then Harper showed Gwen how to fill the horses' water tank just inside the fence by using the hose and spigot outside of the pasture.

"Now let's start on the treasure."

"First, would you give me a tour of your farm?" Gwen pulled a water bottle out of her backpack and took a long drink while Harper drank from the spigot.

"We should look for anything unusual," Gwen said, "like places there might have been buildings."

Harper nodded.

The girls walked around the tractor and barn, the little playhouse, and Harper's house. Then they walked around the garden and back down around the horse pasture and the closest cornfield.

"How big is your farm?" Gwen stopped and wiped sweaty strands of hair out of her face.

"Five hundred acres on this side of the road all the way down to the river, and six hundred on the other side of the road." Harper pointed all around her.

Gwen looked down the long hill, past the corn and soybean fields. It must be nearly a mile down to the river that was hidden by a thick line of trees. Beyond those trees and the river more cropland stretched into the distance.

"Isn't all this great?" Harper said, extending her arms and turning around. "Except for the sad looking crops?"

"Maybe for living and farming," Gwen admitted. "But I see acres and acres and acres of land and no clues where to start looking for your treasure." She checked the clock on her phone. "My mom will be here soon. Let's go back to your house."

The girls trudged back up the hill.

"Can you meet me at the library tomorrow afternoon?" Gwen said. "We can look for information about your land and Basil. My dad can drive you home later."

"He doesn't have to. I can ride my bike in."

"That's a long way on a rock road," Gwen said.

"Only a few miles." Harper shrugged. "And the road's not busy. I could ride my bike in for band camp and go to your house for lunch before we go to the library."

Gwen paused. She wanted to say no, but she didn't see how she could. Maybe she wouldn't be able to keep this partnership secret.

"Yeah, I guess."

"You guess?" Harper said, folding her arms across her chest. "I'm not allowed to go to your house?"

Gwen tried to find something to say. "Well, um, my parents aren't always home during the day, so I'd have to ask them if it's okay."

"Well, ask them," Harper said.

The girls sat in the shade of the front porch. Harper's dog walked over and laid his head on Harper's leg. As Harper pet the dog, her sisters and brother pushed through the front door, followed by Harper's very pregnant mom.

"I kept them inside so they wouldn't be in your way," Mrs. Miller said. "Are you okay with them being out here now?"

Harper looked questioningly at Gwen who nodded.

"Yeah, we're done for the day." Harper sighed.

"Hi, Gwen," Mrs. Miller said. "What did you think of your first lesson?"

"It's harder than I thought it would be." Gwen glanced at Harper who was nodding vigorously.

Mrs. Miller smiled. "You'll get it, but not on the first day." She fanned herself with a kitchen towel. "You two must be thirsty. I'll be back with some water."

"Thanks, Mom," Harper said as her mom went inside.

Harper's siblings ran around to the back yard, followed by the dog.

Gwen leaned forward. "Are you getting a new brother or sister?"

"Brother. In late September. He—" Harper abruptly changed the topic. "Why do you want to go to the library? Shouldn't we pick a place to dig? I thought archeologists dug."

"They do. But they research first to decide where to dig."

"We didn't accomplish much today," Harper said, frowning. "Treasure hunting and riding lessons are both going to take longer than I thought. When's your trail ride?"

"Thirty days from today," Gwen said.

"And school and homework start in thirteen days." Harper groaned. "Then we'll have even less time for hunting and riding."

Gwen twisted her bracelet. She might not have enough time for her plan to work.

FIELD NOTES

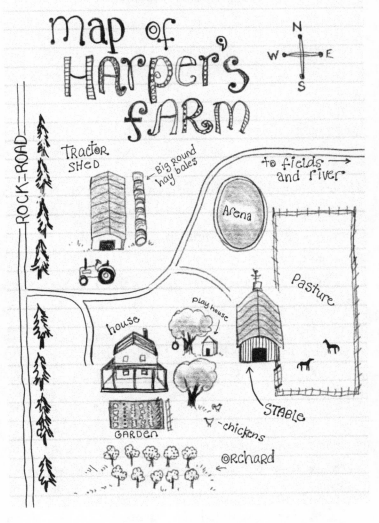

map of
HARper's
fARM

N
W E
S

ROCK=ROAD

TRACTOR
SHED

←Big round
hay bales

to fields →
and river

Arena

Pasture

play house

house

STABLE

GARDEN

↙-chickens

ORCHARD ←

CHAPTER NINE

Friday morning after band practice, Gwen hummed her band music as she put her flute away. She had done a better job keeping in step, and she liked the song they were learning.

Nina, one of the other girls, walked up to Gwen. "We're going to the pool this afternoon. Want to come? Erin's coming too."

Going to the pool sounded wonderful. Gwen could almost feel the cool water. But she had research to do. Did everybody know Erin? Gwen frowned. "Sorry. I can't hang out today. Who's Erin?"

"She moved in next door to Olivia. She and her mom are from Chicago, and her mom is the manager at the new clothing store in the mall."

"Oh." Gwen realized Erin probably liked fashion as much as she and Olivia did. "Is she in our grade?"

"Yeah," Nina said. "Haven't you met her yet? Olivia's been hanging out with her a lot."

Gwen's stomach flip-flopped. Why hadn't Olivia told her about Erin when she'd first gotten to know her?

"Erin's amazing," Nina said. "She knows what's going to be in style before anyone else, and her mom is letting her have a private shopping party for her friends next week. You should come."

"Sounds fun." Gwen waved as Nina walked away. Gwen wondered if this was a real invite to go to the shopping party or if Erin was going to invite her. If she ever met Erin.

Gwen slowly put her flute away. She looked around. A few of the students had left already, but most were still loitering around the school yard. She wished they'd leave before Harper returned from putting her cymbals in the school band room.

No such luck.

Harper pushed her bike up to Gwen. "Want to put your flute case in my basket?"

Gwen shook her head. "It's not heavy." Then a funny thought hit her. "What if you had to take the cymbals in your bike basket to practice at home?"

"My brother would love it!"

Gwen pointed down the sidewalk. "I just live a

couple blocks that way. If you want to ride your bike, you don't have to wait for me."

Harper shrugged as she pushed her bike. "I don't mind."

They walked to Gwen's house. Harper parked her bike outside, and the girls entered the quiet kitchen.

Harper stopped and closed her eyes.

"What's wrong?" Gwen said.

"Nothing," Harper said. "It's so quiet."

"We're the only ones here."

"What's it like living in a quiet house?"

"Nice, I guess. Sometimes a little lonely."

"It's never quiet at my house. There are six of us. And soon there'll be a noisy baby too."

Gwen motioned her down the hall. "I'll put my flute away. Do you want to see my room?"

Harper nodded. "It must be nice to have a whole room to yourself." Harper looked around Gwen's room. "I share with one of my sisters. My sisters and brother always want me to play, they're always into my stuff, and they're always yelling."

"I wish I had a sister or brother." Gwen thought about Di and Clay and Cooper.

"I do love my family but sometimes I hide in the stable." Harper grinned.

"This summer I babysat two little boys that drove me nuts at first," Gwen said, "but I really miss them now. They gave the best hugs. And they didn't care about my clothes or who my friends were. They liked everyone." Gwen remembered her and Olivia's argument about Harper. Her face grew warm.

Gwen quickly looked away, but she also noticed her room with a new perspective. Her mom let her choose the soft yellow color for her wall and pick out her own bedding and curtains. She rearranged the furniture once in a while and traded out the posters on her wall. But it was all hers.

She had never thought her house was anything special. It was a small, rectangular three-bedroom one-level ranch, in a neighborhood filled with houses very similar. Her house was so old that it looked old and dated, but at the same time it was so new it didn't have any historic charm. It was just blah.

She once asked her mom why they lived in such a boring house.

Her mom had replied that she'd rather read about history than deal with old house maintenance. She said their little ranch was just the right size for them —a bedroom for Gwen, a bedroom for her and Gwen's dad, and one that they used for an office.

But the little house did get quiet. Gwen was the only noisy one, and that was only when she played her flute.

Harper peeked out Gwen's window. "I'd hate that," Harper said.

"What?"

"Your neighbor's house is ten feet away. How do you even breathe?"

Gwen thought about the times she heard the sounds of her neighbor's TV or dog. She shrugged. "I'm used to it. Most of the time it doesn't bother me. But when we were at the dig, the sounds of the frogs and coyotes kept me awake. Anyway, let's get some lunch." She led the way back to the kitchen.

The girls ate a couple sandwiches and some carrots, and then both rode their bikes downtown to the library.

What I'd do if I had a sister...

PLAY! -school, house, board games - hide and seek

go to the playground

DO CRAFTS (glitter)

have tea parties

CUDDLE and READ STORIES together

CHAPTER TEN

"Now what?" Harper said.

Gwen scowled. She was most familiar with the kids' area at the library. She looked around the rows of shelves in the main room. She located a seating area that had a few newspapers. But when she approached, she noticed they were newspapers from that day.

She turned around and wondered where old newspapers would be. The library she'd spent lots of time in at Lakeside had a special room for historical stuff, and Mrs. Wagner was always ready to help her. Mrs. Wagner said that's what librarians were for.

"Let's go ask for help." Gwen approached a librarian shelving books. "Excuse me. Where are the old newspapers?"

"We have some paper copies and a few that are online," he replied, "but almost everything has been put on microfiche. Can you tell me what year and which newspaper you'd like?"

"We're researching Harper's family's farm." Gwen turned to Harper. "What year did Basil get the land?"

Harper frowned. "Hmm. I think it was around 1880."

"That narrows it down a little," the librarian said, "because by then Yankton had been in existence for about twenty years. We have microfilm of *The Press and Dakotaian* from that time."

"Could we see that, please?" Gwen asked.

"Sure," the librarian said. "Have you ever used a microfilm machine?"

The girls shook their heads.

"Aren't the newspapers on the Internet?" Harper asked.

"Some are, but not all of them." The librarian smiled. "The best info is not always online."

"I've heard that before," Gwen said, remembering her summer research.

The librarian led the girls to a table that held two machines with large viewing screens. "I'll get a few years of film for you."

He left and returned shortly with a couple boxes

containing the microfilm. Then he showed Gwen and Harper how to thread one of the reels of film in one of the machines.

"Use these controls if you want to move the film forward or backward. If you want to print a page, you press this. But we charge a small fee for every page."

Gwen opened her backpack. "That's okay. I brought notebooks so we can take notes."

"Great! Let me know if you need any help."

Gwen handed a notebook, pen, and a roll of film to Harper. "You take this roll, and I'll search that one. Look for any articles that might mention your family or your land. Look at every page."

The girls quietly looked through the old newspapers for the next hour or so.

Finally, Gwen sat back and rubbed her eyes. "This is starting to give me a headache. All I'm finding are lots of articles about gold mining in the Black Hills, railroads, steamboats and wrecks, and flooding and blizzards. Lots of blizzards. Did you know the winter of 1880–81 is the one Laura Ingalls Wilder wrote about in her book *The Long Winter*? And then that spring Yankton had a huge flood?"

When Harper didn't respond, Gwen turned to see her squinting at her microfilm screen.

"Gwen," Harper whispered. "I found something."

Gwen scooted her chair next to Harper and looked where she pointed.

Harper read aloud:

Mrs. B.F. Miller, along with her five children and a thoroughbred racehorse, arrived in Yankton by train to reunite with her husband at their new farm along the James River, only to learn that he had succumbed to illness and begun his Eternal Journey while the family was en route from England.

The enterprising wife took the tragic news with a great deal of dignity, and instead of retreating back to the Old Country to the comforts of her family, she has decided to stay and make a success of her recently deceased husband's venture.

The Millers' property consists of forty acres, ten of which are newly planted in corn, a well, a shanty, a barn, and two horses.

No doubt the grieving but determined widow will find assistance and comfort through her children and through her new neighbors who have selflessly cared for the late man's crops and livestock.

Harper turned to Gwen with wide eyes.

"B.F. Miller is Basil. That's my family."

"How sad," Gwen said. "Can you imagine what that was like to come all this way and then find out he had died?"

"I didn't know he died before his family got here. How did his family know about the fortune?"

"Maybe he had written them a letter," Gwen said. "It would be really cool if your family still had letters from—what was the date?" She checked the newspaper article. "June 1881. What else does it say?"

"Just that." Harper pushed back from the table. "I'm tired. This has nothing to do with the treasure."

"It's our first clue. Besides, we only know when Basil's wife and children arrived." Gwen recorded the info in her notebook. "We don't know when Basil arrived. We need more clues. Your farm is more than one thousand acres. There's no way we could even start to narrow down where to look if we don't find more clues, like where the original forty acres are."

"By the river."

"Which part of the river? Where was Basil's shanty? Could it have been where your house is now?"

Harper shook her head. "I don't know. My grandparents built our house when my dad was little."

"Where did your grandparents live before they built your house? I didn't see any other houses."

Harper hesitated before speaking. "There's an old shack down on a small rise surrounded by cottonwoods near the river. The Miller family lived in it for a long time. It never had electricity or plumbing, and it's falling down. I've peeked in it but there isn't anything inside it."

"Why didn't you say so before? That's probably it."

"Because it's not Basil's shanty, either. Dad says it was ordered from a catalog and put together in the 1920s."

"You could order a house? Who knew?" Gwen frowned. "But that was a long time after Basil died. It would be too late."

"Maybe the 1920s house was built near the shanty. The article said Basil's farm was along the river. The 1920s house is pretty close to the river," Harper said.

"That would make sense because they'd still be close to their well and their barn." Gwen twirled the end of her ponytail around a finger as she thought out loud. "If the treasure was inside the first shanty, someone would've found it. What if it was under the shanty and then got covered by dirt? My friend, Di, found a thimble she thinks was lost *under* a house. We could start down by the 1920s house and use the metal detector and see what we can find."

"Who's Di?"

"She was one of the college students who was at our dig this summer. She's the one who invited me on the trail ride. She's going into the Army soon, so the ride might be my last chance to see her." Gwen swallowed.

"So she's the reason you want to ride even though you're terrified of horses?"

Gwen nodded. "Di was a good friend to me even when I wasn't to her."

"Sappy." Harper laughed.

"Yeah, but nice." Gwen looked away. "Some of my other friends haven't been that great lately." Gwen thought of Olivia and how she didn't seem to care about what was happening in Gwen's life or what Gwen liked anymore. Good thing Di still cared.

"Can you come out now to ride and dig?" Harper said.

Gwen checked the time and shook her head. "My family is going to do a picnic at the lake this evening. Besides, my mom said we have to get permission from your parents before we dig. They have to make sure there aren't any buried wires or pipes."

Harper nodded. "I have polo practice tomorrow morning, so we'll have to wait until after lunch." She closed her notebook and handed it to Gwen. "Tomorrow we find the treasure."

"Archeology doesn't happen in a day," Gwen said.

"Don't be such a downer."

Gwen bit her lip as she took her reel of film off the viewer. Harper was expecting too much, and she was going to be really frustrated when they didn't find buried gold. She was setting them up to fail.

FIELD NOTES...
from the library

DAKOTA Territory 1880-1881

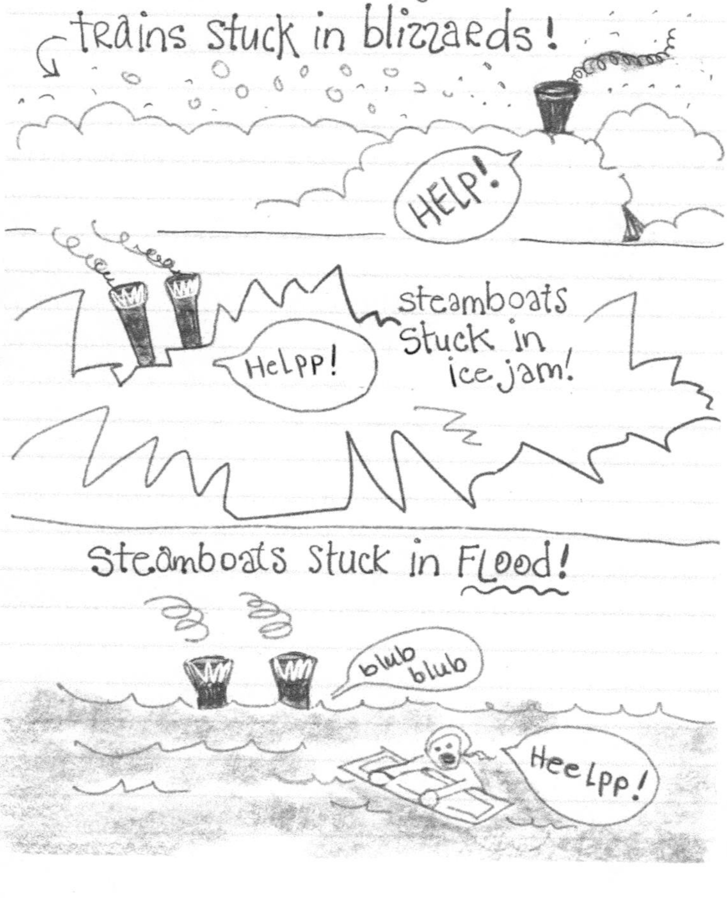

CHAPTER ELEVEN

Saturday afternoon, Gwen's dad drove Gwen out to Harper's farm. "You look prepared for anything," he said.

Gwen had dressed in blue jeans and her hiking boots. Her backpack held her phone, a water bottle, her notebook, a pen, a bunch of little flags on wires, her hat, and sunscreen. She had also packed her trowel, a hand spade that had jagged edges for cutting into the sod, a paintbrush, and two pairs of gloves into a big bucket. Plus, she had the metal detector in the back seat of the car.

"You do have permission to dig, right?" her dad said.

"Harper checked with her parents, and they said there've never been any pipes or wires down by the river. And the well was plugged."

"Good." He nodded. "Call when you're ready to be picked up."

"Thanks for the ride." Gwen hopped out of the car and unloaded all her equipment.

Harper came out to meet her.

"Harper! Play with us!" Harper's sisters and brother hurtled themselves from the house toward Harper.

"I can't now," Harper said. "I've got work to do with Gwen."

The kids turned to Gwen and looked at her quietly.

"Hi," Gwen said, waving. "What are your names? What are you playing?"

"We're going to storm the castle," the oldest girl said. She pointed to herself and the other children. "I'm Bea, and I'm eight. This is Rhys. He's seven. And Lily's five."

"What's storm the castle?" Gwen asked.

"It's like capture the flag," Rhys said. "And our playhouse is the castle."

"We need more people," Bea said.

"That sounds like fun." Gwen smiled. Clay and Cooper would love that game.

"No." Harper shook her head. "I want to get down to the 1920s house before it gets too hot."

"Please? Please? Please?" The children jumped up

and down.

Gwen gave Harper her best puppy dog eyes.

Harper glared at Gwen. "Really?"

Gwen nodded.

Harper softened. "Work first. Then maybe we'll play." She turned to her siblings. "But you have to promise me that you won't follow us."

The kids nodded.

Gwen gave them each a high-five.

Then Gwen and Harper grabbed the metal detector and the rest of Gwen's gear, and Harper also carried a hand scythe. They walked down the hill through tall grass past a cornfield and a soybean field.

Gwen searched for snakes as she took each step.

After walking about fifteen minutes, Gwen put down the detector and fanned herself with her hat. "It's already too hot." She dreaded the walk back, especially lugging all the equipment.

"When you learn to ride, we'll take the horses," Harper said.

When they reached the trees near the river, they turned and hiked up a small hill, entering a clearing where a weathered wooden shell of a building nestled in the weeds. The old house leaned to one side, and the broken window glass gave it a sad appearance.

"Dad will ground me for life if I go inside. But it's

safe outside. My dad and his brother used to camp down here when they were kids."

Gwen looked around. "Another house or houses could've been just about anywhere here. I don't think anyone would've lived in a shanty very long. Shanties were just tiny shacks. People added on to them or built nicer houses. I've seen photos of old shanties that were smaller than the Ark."

"The Ark?" Harper frowned.

"Our motorhome," Gwen said. "I call it the Archeology-mobile. The Ark, for short."

Gwen noticed an L-shaped line of overgrown bushes that bordered two sides of the clearing. "See those bushes, how they're in a straight line?"

"Yeah."

"Maybe they made a windbreak for a house."

"Those are lilacs. They're covered in purple flowers in the spring. I like to come down to cut some of the branches to bring to my mom."

"Lilacs!" Gwen clapped her hands. "People used lilacs around their yards and houses, and they can live a long time."

"More than a hundred years?"

"I don't know." Gwen shrugged. "But I bet one of your great-grandmothers planted them. Let's use the metal detector between the house and the lilacs. Maybe the shanty was in between them."

"Okay," Harper said. "I'll cut down some of these weeds so we have room to walk and use the detector."

Harper went to work with the scythe.

While she was doing that, Gwen organized her tools. Harper finished up one small area and took a water break while Gwen paced off the cleared area and stuck a flag into the ground every five steps.

"What are you doing?"

"Making our square units."

The girls continued cutting weeds and making squares until they had a large area cleared and marked.

Then Gwen showed Harper how to use the detector.

"It's almost like we're waving a magic wand over the ground. Work in just one unit at a time. Keep the coil close to the ground, and go really slow."

While Harper was sweeping the first unit, Gwen turned the bucket upside down, sat on it, and drew a map of the clearing in her notebook.

"Why are you doing that?" Harper asked.

"I can put a star on the map wherever we find something. If we find a bunch of nails that are in a square or rectangle pattern, then maybe we found the house. And if we don't find anything in a unit, I can cross out the unit on the map so we don't waste time going over the same parts."

"Oh. Smart."

Gwen looked at Harper and smiled. It was the first time Harper had complimented her.

The girls took turns sweeping the units and slowly crossed off squares.

On the last row, Harper said, "Are you sure we're doing this right?" Just then the detector started beeping. "Hey, I found something!"

Gwen pulled out the spade with the cutting edges and dug where the beeping was fastest and strongest.

"I'm just barely getting through the soil." Gwen grunted and pushed the spade into the hard soil. "I think we need a regular shovel." She put her weight on the spade and felt a clod of earth move. She kept working and pulled a crumpled can out of the dirt. She wiped it off and showed it to Harper.

"An old soda can," Harper exclaimed.

Gwen tossed it on the ground. "They didn't have soda in cans in 1880. It's just trash." She remembered her parents' dig. "My parents find some of the best stuff in places where trash was buried." Gwen shuddered. "Or in old privy pits. That's kind of like a treasure stash for archeologists. If we could find where the trash was buried or the privy pit was, maybe we could find a clue."

"What's a privy pit?"

"It's the filled-in hole from an outhouse."

Harper stared at her. "Funny. What is it really?"

"That's the truth."

"Old poop?"

Gwen nodded.

"Who would put a treasure in a poop pit? How would you get it back out?"

"Nobody would think to look there." Gwen stood and brushed the dirt off her knees.

"Maybe they would. I saw a TV show where a bad guy hid evidence in a toilet, and that was the first place the police looked." Harper stood and put her hands on her hips.

"Would you rather stick your hand in a toilet or in an outhouse pit?"

"The toilet," Harper admitted. "If Basil put it in the pit, how do you think he planned to get it out?"

"Maybe he had it wrapped in some kind of water-proofed leather. Or in a metal box. And maybe he'd attached it to a rope so he could pull it out—like a rope on a bucket in a well."

"How do we find the trash or privy pit? Got a poop detector?"

"Don't be ridiculous. People often threw trash—including old metal—into the privy pits. But if the shanty was here, they wouldn't have put an ugly, stinky outhouse near it, and definitely not in their front yard." Gwen slowly turned around. "I suppose the front would face the road."

"What road?" Harper voice rose as she waved an arm.

"Yeah, I don't see one. But there must have been some kind of road or driveway." Gwen paced as she thought. "Let's go back to the library tomorrow and look for an old map."

"All right. But now it's time for you to ride Ruby."

As Gwen pictured herself sitting on Ruby's back, her shoulders drooped. She wished she were braver.

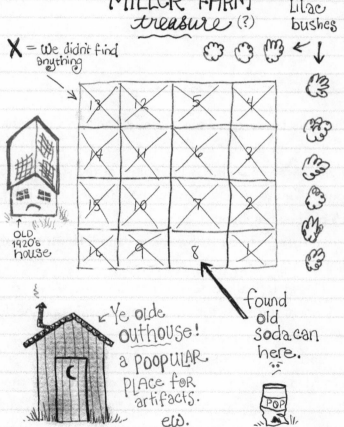

CHAPTER TWELVE

The girls trudged up the hill and back to the stable. They stored all the tools in the tack room and took another water break. Gwen looked at the soles on her boots. They were chunky, so she changed into Harper's old cowboy boots.

Harper grabbed Ruby's halter and lead off a hook. "Let's get going."

The girls walked to the pasture gate. "You shut and open the gate for me," Harper said as she let herself into the pasture.

Both horses walked up to Harper, and she rewarded them with pieces of carrot. "Not this time, Boots." Harper patted the horse's shoulder and pushed her away. Then she put the halter on Ruby and led her through the gate that Gwen opened and shut.

Harper handed the lead to Gwen. "Take her to the crossties."

Gwen obeyed, careful to keep far enough to Ruby's left so the horse wouldn't accidentally step on her toes. Gwen hooked up Ruby and removed the lead. "Now what?"

"We start with a light grooming to remove the dirt so it doesn't irritate Ruby's skin under the blanket and saddle. Also, check her over in case she got scratched or has anything prickly in her fur."

"Your horses get groomed almost as much as I do," Gwen said, looking down at her dirty clothes. She was ready for a shower herself.

"They can't do it themselves," Harper said. "If you want to ride them, you take good care of them. Besides, it's fun. And it'll help you and Ruby keep getting to know each other." She went into the tack room.

Gwen swallowed. She was going to do this.

"Are you staying cool, Ruby? Bet your fur is hot." She held out her palm to let Ruby smell her. "We're trying this riding thing again. I'll try to cowgirl up. Harper says you're the gentlest horse in the neighborhood. But Boots is the only other horse around."

Gwen brushed both sides of Ruby's neck and back.

Harper made a couple trips out of the tack room

to bring out the blanket, saddle, bridle, and reins. She hefted the saddle and blanket to the top of the stall's half side wall and then hung the bridle on a hook.

"Now her hooves." Harper handed Gwen the hoof pick.

Gwen gulped. She took the pick in her right hand, slid her left one down Ruby's front leg like Harper had shown her, and squeezed the horse's lower leg.

Ruby lifted her hoof.

Gwen leaned down and grabbed it with her left. "Her foot's so heavy." Gwen struggled to hold the hoof steady.

"Slide your hand closer to the edge of the hoof. There. Now use the pick and clean out the gunk."

Gwen got a whiff of the manure packed into Ruby's hoof. She gagged. It was the worst thing she'd ever smelled, and it was inches from her face. While holding her breath, Gwen scraped the manure away from the horseshoe and out of the indentations of Ruby's hoof.

"You'll get it as you practice, but I'll do the rest," Harper said, taking the pick. "Don't want you all worn out before we get started."

Gwen retreated to the side of Ruby's head and stroked the horse's muzzle while Harper finished with the hooves. "It must be nice to get a pedicure every day."

"Don't you take care of your feet?" Harper said as she swept the manure and dirt and stones to the side of the stall. "If you had a stone in your shoe, you'd take it out. See if you can put the blanket, saddle, and bridle on her yourself. I'll get your helmet."

Gwen lifted the saddle blanket over Ruby's back. That was the easy part. "I don't even know if I can lift your saddle. Help me out, Ruby. No kicking."

Harper came back with the helmet. She leaned against the wall. "Ruby's not going to kick you if you stay away from her back feet. Remember, if you're acting scared, she's going to get nervous. If you're calm and confident, she'll trust you."

Gwen wasn't confident, but she could act confident. "Here goes." She heaved the saddle above her head and eased it onto the horse's back, then Gwen reached under Ruby's belly to grab the cinch. She stared at the strap. What was the next step?

Harper came over and showed her how to loop the strap and fasten it. Then Harper handed the bit and bridle to Gwen.

Gwen felt the horse drool on her hand and grimaced. She realized she was going to have to touch drool a lot. There was no place to clean her hand, so she sighed and wiped it on her jeans.

In the arena, Harper lined up Ruby to the step stool and held the horse still. "Ready?"

Gwen climbed the stool. She looked at the saddle and grabbed the reins and a handful of mane. She hesitated and then stuck her left foot in the stirrup.

"One, two, three," Gwen counted and then launched herself up throwing her right leg over Ruby's back. "I did it!" Gwen leaned and patted Ruby's right shoulder. Then she felt herself tipping to the right. Her body—and the saddle—was slowly sliding over Ruby's side.

"Help!" Gwen clung to Ruby's mane as she hung cockeyed on the horse.

Laughing, Harper grabbed Gwen's foot with one hand and the cinch strap with the other.

"Quit laughing and help me!" Gwen yelled.

Harper let go of Gwen's leg and grabbed her arm, pulling both her and the saddle into an upright position. She held the saddle steady as Gwen dismounted.

Gwen wobbled. "It's not funny!"

"If you say so," Harper said. "But you did get on by yourself. The only thing is that you forgot to tighten the cinch. After Ruby first walks a few steps, the strap might shift. You *always* need to check it before you mount her."

"You knew that would happen. That was mean!"

"I wasn't going to let you fall." Harper pulled hard on the strap. "You'll never forget again. Now get back up there."

Gwen glared at Harper. She willed herself to breathe slow, stop shaking, and get back into the saddle.

Harper shortened the stirrups to a length that was comfortable for Gwen's legs.

"See how your boots feel locked into the stirrup when your heels are down?" Harper said. "Soon you'll be able to talk to her with your knees and legs."

"What?" Gwen said, pushing her heels down further. "I thought that's what the bit and reins were for."

"They're your back-up system. Your legs are more important, at least for now." Then Harper demonstrated how to hold the reins in her right hand. "Let's go for a walk."

Gwen tried to focus on relaxing and holding the reins correctly. She looked at the ground. It was still a long way down! She felt herself get dizzy and forced herself to look above Ruby's ears.

Harper showed Gwen how to push her leg against the horse's side to "ask" Ruby to turn in the direction she was nudging the horse toward, how to reinforce the change of direction with the reins, and how to cue Ruby to stop and start.

Harper walked next to Ruby's head as they went around the arena a couple times. She also had her stop and start Ruby multiple times. Harper backed away a few steps and stood still as Ruby kept walking around the arena. "Sit up straight, keep your heels down, relax, and let your body move as she moves."

As Ruby stopped and started a few times on command, and as she walked slowly, Gwen began to relax and feel the rhythm of Ruby's gait. Her body began to move with the horse.

The breeze wafted horse odor around her, but it also cooled her off. She smiled. The smell wasn't so bad.

She was actually riding. What had she been so scared of?

FIELD NOTES
How to ride a horse

in your dreams!

1. **GROOM.** Brush ▭ curry comb ⚬ pick "gunk" out of hooves. → manure

2. **Put on** saddle blanket ▭ & **saddle** → & tighten **cinch** strap →

3. wiggle **Bit** into horse's mouth and put on **Bridle.** → *eww.* —slobber

4. **TIGHTEN CINCH!** again.

5. mount. **Get on the horse.** YEEHAW!

6. Put feet in **Stirrups.** Keep heels down!

7. Hold **reins** in **Right** hand. (Western style) Tight enough, but not too tight.

8. Sit up **STRAIGHT,** But *loose?*

9. **Look** ahead. Not at ground.

10. *relax.* (yeah, right!)

CHAPTER THIRTEEN

Sunday afternoon Harper rode her bike to Gwen's house, and the girls rode their bikes to the library. Once inside, Gwen and Harper approached the librarian.

"We're looking for old maps of the area," Gwen said. "Do you have any?"

"Of course," the librarian said.

Soon Gwen and Harper were leafing through a stack of maps.

Gwen tried to focus on the maps and not on the new deadline her parents had given her that morning.

"Here's one from 1881," Harper said.

Gwen studied it. "Well, here's Yankton. So your farm is over here somewhere. See, here's where the James River runs into the Missouri River. Look at this road that runs next to the James."

"Follow that north," Harper said. "Look! There's Basil's name! I think this L-shape is our farm, or at least part of it."

"Do you recognize anything else on this map?"

Harper shook her head. She jumped up and headed toward the table of computers.

Gwen grabbed her notebook and the map and followed her.

Harper opened an online satellite photo of her family farm. "We can compare the map with the satellite photo that shows my house, the 1920s house, and the river."

"You're getting the hang of this."

"Maybe not." Harper pointed at the screen. "Here's the 1920s house, but the river doesn't look the same as on the 1881 map. It's actually closer to the house than it was in the 1880s."

"My dad says the river changes its path over time because of erosion, floods, and even earthquakes."

"It looks like the 1881 road cuts across where we were working yesterday," Harper said.

"Then we need to search closer to the river." Gwen opened her notebook. "I'm going to draw a map combining the old one and the satellite photo. That'll be our master map."

"What are you going to do about the different river paths?"

"I'll make the newer one with a solid line and the older one with a dotted line."

"If we're done here, let's ride out to my house. You've got a lot to learn if you plan to go on that pack trip in less than a month."

"Less than that." Gwen sighed. "My parents want to watch me ride on Friday. They want to see what I've learned before they give me the okay and make plans for the trip."

"Learn to ride in five days? That's almost impossible. But we're going to try."

—

At the farm, Gwen rode Ruby around the arena.

Harper stood in the center and gave Gwen directions. She'd have her direct Ruby one way around the arena, cut across the middle, and then go in the opposite direction.

Gwen and Ruby worked for about forty-five minutes. Gwen felt like she was starting to get the hang of steering.

"That's enough for today," Harper said.

"I have time to do more before my dad picks me up," Gwen said.

"Trust me. If you don't stop, you're going to regret it later."

"What do you mean?"

"Your legs and rear will be too sore and then you won't want to ride. You only have five more riding days. You can't afford to skip any."

"Oh."

"Want to see how to really ride?"

"Sure!"

The girls took care of Ruby's after-lesson grooming and turned her out into the pasture. Harper grabbed Boots, walked her to the crossties, groomed and saddled her, wrapped the lower part of her legs, and started to braid Boots' tail.

"So polo horses—ponies—are into looking good too?" Gwen said.

"The wraps are for protection and the braiding is so mallets don't get tangled in their tails. But when we're not playing, they need their tails to brush away flies, so we don't trim them like we do the manes."

"I'm good at braiding," Gwen said.

"You could do Ruby's tail sometime." Harper doubled Boots' tail on itself and tied it off with some loose pieces of Boots' tail hair.

Harper grabbed her helmet, gloves, mallet, and a small plastic ball from the tack room and handed them to Gwen. Then the girls walked Boots to the arena.

Gwen opened the gate for Harper and Boots. "A

braided tail is part of her polo uniform. What's your uniform?"

"Helmet, goggles, gloves, knee guards, team shirt, tall boots, and white breeches."

"White pants? Don't they get dirty?"

"That's what bleach is for." Harper put on her helmet and mounted Boots. "It's tradition."

"Well, that fashion decision's not very practical."

"You're choosing practical over stylish? I'm shocked."

"Ha-ha."

"Athletes in lots of sports wear white. Football. Baseball. Cricket. Tennis." Harper talked while she trotted Boots around the arena.

"What do people wear for trail rides?"

"Those aren't competitions, so just practical clothes: long pants, long socks so your boots don't chafe your legs all day, gloves, and then whatever you need to be warm enough or cool enough or dry enough."

"What do you mean dry enough?" Gwen furrowed her brow.

"If you're out there for a week, you've got to be prepared to get rained on. And nights get cold." Harper asked Boots to change directions.

"How do you know all this?" Gwen said.

"We've done family trail rides in the Black Hills."

"Oh." Gwen frowned. Harper was such a know-it-all. But Gwen was also surprised at herself. Planning her outfits would usually be the first thing she did before going somewhere. But not this time.

"I can't believe I'm going to ask this, but sometime, would you go with me to the western store downtown and show me what you think I might need?"

Harper stopped Boots in front of Gwen and grinned. "Oh, the irony! You wanted to help me with my style."

Gwen's face burned. "Don't rub it in!"

"That sounds fun," Harper said, laughing. "Now put the ball on the ground and hand me my mallet, and then you need to go on the other side of the fence."

Harper held the reins in her left hand and swung the mallet with her right hand. She leaned over Boots' side and hit the ball up and down the arena as Boots trotted or cantered.

Gwen was impressed. Harper and Boots seemed to be part of each other. Harper moved with the horse, and she hardly seemed to give the horse direction, yet she was in total control. How did she stay on? Harper's polo saddle didn't have a saddle horn like Gwen's did. Harper had said the polo saddle was an English-style saddle.

Harper thought for the trail rides in Colorado, they would probably supply western tack, so Gwen was using a western-style saddle. Even her bit, bridle, stirrups, and reins were different than what Harper used for polo.

After Harper was done practicing, she walked Boots around the corral for a while to let the horse cool down. Then she dismounted and led Boots to the crossties where she took off all the tack, undid her tail, and brushed her well, giving her more time to cool down.

"That was a lot of work for fifteen minutes of riding," Gwen said as Harper led Boots back into the pasture.

"Boots had practice yesterday." Harper petted Boots' nose before releasing her. "I didn't want to overwork her."

"You just wanted to show off," Gwen said.

"True." Harper fastened the gate shut. "But your lessons are eating into my riding time. You can add some fresh water to the stock tank now."

Gwen's back stiffened. "You're not the only one sacrificing time for our deal."

Harper planted herself in front of Gwen. "Making a deal was your idea. Remember? Add water to the stock tank. I'm going to get a bucket to water the cats." She swaggered into the stable.

Gwen grumbled as she fed the end of the hose between the fence rungs into the tank and turned on the water spigot.

Harper returned with a bucket and set it on the ground in front of her. "Spray some water in here."

"Yes, ma'am," Gwen muttered. She grabbed the end of the hose and held it as the water gushed into the bucket. When it was nearly full, she lifted the end of the hose into the air—without thinking about what she was doing—and sprayed water all over Harper's waist and legs.

Harper gasped.

FIELD NOTES

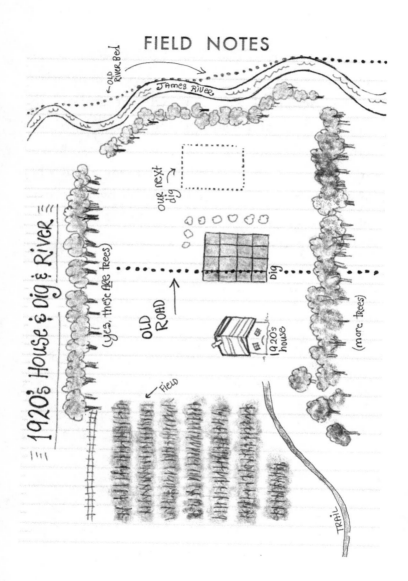

CHAPTER FOURTEEN

Gwen stood frozen, watching the water soak Harper. She shook herself and quickly put the end of the hose into the bucket at Harper's feet.

"I'm so sorry," Gwen said. "I didn't mean to do that."

Harper scowled at her. Then she leaned over and put her hands on her knees.

Gwen couldn't see her face and wondered if Harper was angry. What if she'd made her cry?

"Harper?" Gwen kneeled down to see Harper's face. "Are you okay? I didn't mean to get you wet."

Suddenly, Harper grabbed the bucket and splashed water into Gwen's face.

Gwen choked on the water in her mouth, and the shock of the cold water running down her neck and inside her shirt sent a shiver down her back.

Harper laughed like a superhero villain and splashed Gwen again.

Gwen screamed, running away in a zigzag pattern, grabbed the hose, and aimed in Harper's direction.

Harper heaved the rest of the bucket water at Gwen, drenching her.

"Girls!"

Harper and Gwen turned at the sound of Harper's mom.

"That's the animals' water!" Mrs. Miller stood with her hands on her hips.

Gwen's dad stood next to her, his arms across his chest, studying his fingernails. But his shoulders shook slightly. Gwen knew he was trying not to laugh.

"I was going to offer you two some ice cream to cool you down before Gwen went home, but I'd say you were cool enough. Make sure you cool down the horses." Mrs. Miller winked at Harper and then headed back to the house. "Dr. Bell, would you like some ice cream while the girls finish up here?"

"Yes, please!" Gwen's dad followed Harper's mom. "Gwen's going to need to dry off a bit before she gets in my car."

Gwen walked stiff-legged back to the water spigot. Her wet jeans clung to her legs, and water dripped down her back. She wrung the water out of her shirttail and watched Harper refill her bucket.

Harper wiped a wet strand of hair out of her face and looked at Gwen.

Both girls burst into laughter.

—

When Gwen got home that evening, she showered and changed. Then she practiced her marching band songs on her flute. She'd mastered *The Star-Spangled Banner*.

Gwen's phone rang. It was Olivia.

"What's up?" Gwen's stomach flip-flopped. Olivia usually texted instead of calling. "Is everything okay?"

"Yeah," Olivia said. "But since Mom made me put my phone away for the whole trip, I had too much to tell you for just texting."

"Oh." Gwen realized she hadn't even noticed that it had been four days since she'd last talked to Olivia. She'd really missed Olivia most of the summer, but now she'd been so busy with band camp and Harper that she barely realized Olivia was away. Weird. "How was vacation?"

"Same old, same old," Olivia said. "Except Mom took us to a rodeo. She said it would be fun. It was two hours of kids roping calves. I about heaved from the smell."

Gwen swallowed. She sniffed her damp hair and

hoped it didn't smell like horse. She'd become used to the smell and now couldn't tell if she carried the odor with her. She changed the subject. "Did you get your school outfits figured out?"

"I've got lots of ideas. We have to go window-shopping! How about tomorrow afternoon?"

"Umm," Gwen said, stalling. "I can't. How about Saturday?"

"Can't. My new neighbor is having a party. Don't you have a free afternoon before then?"

"Is that Erin?" Gwen paused again. She gripped her phone and frowned.

"Yeah," Olivia said. "So when can you get together?"

Gwen had plans for every day, but she didn't want to explain why. Finally she laid the blame with her mom. "I have to check with my mom first."

Olivia was silent for a long minute. "Fine. If you don't want to hang out, just say so." She hung up.

Gwen sat on her bed and stared at her phone. She would like to see Olivia and her ideas for new outfits, but she also wanted to see Di. That meant riding lessons. And Olivia wouldn't get it. Gwen wished she could tell her about the lessons and getting the chance to do her own archeological dig.

Olivia wouldn't like Gwen spending time with

Harper, either. Olivia had made it clear that she wasn't going to give Harper a chance.

Gwen just needed another five lessons to show her parents she could handle the trail ride. Then she'd see Di, and if she never patched things up with Olivia, she'd still have Di's friendship.

Gwen sighed. Her room felt empty, and her house was quiet even though her parents were in the living room. She put her flute away. Then she went to the bathroom to pick up her wet, dirty clothes off the floor. She was going to need them tomorrow for digging and riding, so she might as well throw them in the washing machine.

She sniffed the clothes. The smell of horse triggered memories of that afternoon: researching at the library, riding Ruby, laughing with Harper. It had been a fun day.

Gwen pushed away her thoughts about Olivia. She couldn't wait for tomorrow.

FIELD NOTES

CHAPTER FIFTEEN

Monday morning at band camp, Gwen sat with the group of girls waiting for the marching to begin and watched out of the corner of her eye for Harper's arrival.

Soon, Harper's truck pulled up next to the curb. She slid out of the truck and lifted her bike out of the back end. Then she slowly pushed her bike to the bike rack and trudged to her tree. She glanced at Gwen and then looked away quickly, wiping at an eye with her hand.

Was she crying? Gwen wondered if she should go over and ask her what's wrong. In front of the other girls? She looked back at Harper. She was sitting with her back against the tree with a book in front of her face.

Oh, well, Gwen thought. Harper obviously didn't want to talk now. Gwen would ask her about it this afternoon.

—

After band camp, Gwen walked stiffly while Harper rode her bike to Gwen's house.

"Why are you walking funny?" Harper said.

"My legs are sore," Gwen said.

"Aren't you glad I didn't let you ride longer yesterday?"

Gwen nodded. Maybe yesterday is why Harper looked upset. "Did you get in trouble with your mom after I left?"

"About the water?" Harper said. "Not really. The heat makes her grumpy, and she's always hot right now. And she doesn't want me wasting water, or anything. She's always talking about bills. The electrical bill, the water bill, the doctor's bill, the lesson bill—" Harper pressed her lips together.

"What's wrong?" Gwen said.

"Nothing." Harper stammered. "If we don't find the treasure today, we at least need to find a really good clue."

"Archeology can be super slow," Gwen said. "It

took us a long time before we found anything at our dig this summer."

"If we could just find something . . ." Harper fell silent.

The girls went to Gwen's house where Gwen left her flute, changed into her digging/riding clothes, and got her backpack. They ate sandwiches and then biked out to Harper's farm.

Once at the farm, Harper stood in the middle of the arena and had Gwen repeat all the exercises with Ruby she'd already learned.

But Gwen mixed up her steering commands. She felt like she had forgotten what she'd already learned and was now confusing the horse. "I'm not getting this." Gwen frowned.

"It takes practice until you start doing it without thinking about it," Harper said. "Besides, Ruby is smart. She kind of knows what you want even if you mess up."

"How? Does she read minds?" Gwen grumped.

"Yes."

Gwen stared at her. "Seriously?"

"You're gullible." Harper laughed, snorting. "No, but she can read your body language. If you've turned your head and shoulders a certain direction, she thinks that's the way you want to go. See?"

Gwen realized that the horse had wandered into

the center of the arena toward Harper because Gwen had turned her shoulders toward Harper.

After working with Ruby for about forty-five minutes, the girls took care of the horse and turned her out in the pasture where Boots was nibbling grass. Then they walked down to the 1920s house. Gwen carried her backpack, the metal detector, and a full-size shovel, and Harper carried the scythe and the bucket with the rest of their gear.

They cut down weeds on the other side of the lilacs until they reached the trees, and then they marked square units and used the metal detector in all the new units.

Gwen was sipping water and drawing lines through the units she'd added to the map in her notebook while Harper ran the detector.

Suddenly the detector began beeping.

Gwen looked up and met Harper's eyes.

As Harper moved the detector, the beeping came louder and faster.

Gwen jumped up and ran to Harper. She kicked at the grass under the detector to see if she could see anything. Nothing.

Harper stepped on the full-sized spade to cut the tough sod. When she removed a clod, Gwen used the hand spade and joined in digging.

When they got past the roots from the grasses, the

soil became hard so Gwen used her trowel to scrape the soil. Gwen finally pulled up a crushed and burned piece of metal.

"What is it?" Harper said. "Do you think it's a clue?"

Gwen turned it over and over, examining it. "I don't know. It might be some kind of food can. But it's smashed, and it's so burnt you can't see if it had a paper around it or if it had any printing on it."

"Is it important?"

"I don't know." Gwen sat down in the grass. "It's kind of strange that it's burnt. Was there a fire here?"

Harper's eyes widened. "My dad used to burn some of our trash. He said they did that all the time when he was a kid."

"If your ancestors used to burn their trash, maybe we found their trash pile!"

"What now?"

Gwen fingered the artifact as she thought. "We could either dig deeper or keep using the metal detector to see if there's another, or better, place to dig."

"Let's do both. I'll dig, and you detect."

"Okay." Gwen swept the detector around the hole where Harper dug.

The detector went off a couple more times, and

Gwen stuck a flag in the soil to mark the places to dig later.

"Hey," Harper said. "I found something."

Gwen peeked into the hole. At the bottom was a small tube-like shape. "Let's widen the hole to see what it is."

The girls worked together.

"I hope this means we found the trash pit," Harper said.

"Don't get too excited," Gwen warned. "Even if it's the trash pit, it doesn't mean we've found your treasure."

"I can hope."

Gwen handed a paintbrush to Harper. "Use this to brush the soil off the artifact." Gwen retrieved her phone and notebook.

Harper began to pick up the item.

"Stop!" Gwen said. "Put it back where it was. Gently."

"What?" Harper said. "Don't you want to see it?"

"After I take photos and draw a sketch."

"Why?"

"That's what archeologists do with artifacts before they take them out of their unit. They also see if there's other stuff nearby. I should've done that with the burnt metal."

"Why?"

"It helps them see if other artifacts they find might be from the same time period, or even the same people. And they always take notes so they can look back later at the details that they might forget."

"This isn't a real archeology dig."

"Why not? We're trying to find out more about your ancestors."

"Have it your way." Harper waited, bouncing her foot while Gwen sketched and photographed the object. "Now can I pick it up?"

"Go ahead."

Harper picked up the object and held it in her palm. It was a green glass bottle. She turned it over. "It's broken and filled with dirt."

"Look," Gwen said, pointing at some ridges at the top of the bottle. "It must have had a screw-on lid, and there's also some sort of design in the sides that the dirt is packed into."

She took the paintbrush and brushed off more of the dirt. "Pour some water from your water bottle over it."

Harper did, and Gwen wiped it with her shirttail.

"See the design? It has lines that make a pattern like our grids."

Harper looked closer. "So?"

"If I show this to my mom, she might be able to use the pattern to figure out who made it and when.

Then we'd have an idea of how old this trash pit is. If it's a trash pit."

"It is. I know it." Harper stood up and did a little dance. "This clue means we're getting closer to the treasure!"

FIELD NOTES

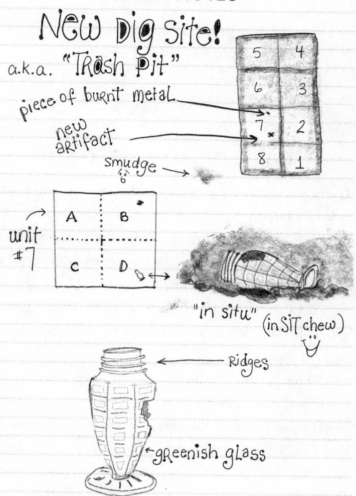

New Dig Site!
a.k.a. "Trash Pit"

5	4
6	3
7	2
8	1

piece of burnt metal

new artifact

smudge →

unit #7

| A | B |
| C | D |

"in situ" (in SIT chew)

Ridges

greenish glass

CHAPTER SIXTEEN

Gwen watched Harper's happy dance. This was a new side of Harper. Mostly she was sarcastic and focused on work. This "treasure" must be really important to her to go to all this trouble and to get excited about an old broken bottle. But why?

"Let's celebrate!" Harper stopped dancing and grinned. "We're out of ice cream, so let's go to town and get some."

"What about finding your treasure as soon as possible?" Gwen said.

Harper brushed the dirt off her jeans. "A lesson should always end with a win. And we won't know a date for that artifact until you talk to your mom. Besides, we can look for your trail riding clothes."

"Hooray! But we're sweaty and filthy." Gwen sniffed her shirt. "Whew! And stinky."

"We'll change before we leave. You can wear something of mine. Besides, it's August. Everyone's hot and smelly."

The girls packed up their equipment and started up the hill back to Harper's house.

Gwen fanned herself with her hat. "This hill goes on forever."

"Especially lugging all this stuff," Harper said, tipping her head. "Tomorrow we'll ride the horses down here."

"Really?" Gwen turned to her. "Do you think I'm ready?"

"We'll just walk them. You are more comfortable around Ruby. You might not feel ready, but you've got to get out of the arena sometime. Especially if you're going to trail ride backcountry."

Harper spoke the truth. Gwen was going to have to learn to ride on a trail, not just in an arena —and although she was frustrated that she wasn't learning as quickly as she wanted to, she was improving.

"I guess you're a good teacher," Gwen said.

"Of course I am." Harper grinned. Then she shrugged. "You've turned out to be a good archeologist."

Gwen smiled. She realized she was feeling comfortable with Harper too. Like she did with Di.

And maybe she was just more comfortable — or confident — with herself.

—

The girls biked to the western store. Gwen wore a pair of Harper's too-small jeans and a boxy t-shirt that sported a seed company logo, as well as her own hiking boots.

"Don't buy anything," Harper said. "We'll just look, and I can show you the types of clothes you'll need. I'll be *your* personal stylist. Then you can buy some things at the thrift store so you'll have money to buy the things you'll really need to be new, like long wool socks and the right kind of sleeping bag."

"You sound just like —" Gwen stopped before she said, "Olivia." Harper may not like Olivia, but her suggestions were exactly how Olivia shopped. To stretch her money, Olivia looked at new clothes online and in stores, then she'd buy second-hand basics and a few new trendy items. Olivia was good at shopping, and Gwen was good at putting outfits together. They made a good team.

The girls wandered around the store, with Harper pointing out certain items like long-sleeved shirts, gloves, vests, jackets, and rain gear.

"Do you think I'll need a hat?" Gwen pointed to the display of cowboy hats.

Harper tipped her head. "You better stick to your helmet. I always wear one." Harper shrugged. "A safe head is better than a pretty head."

"True," Gwen said. "But look, there's a pink one. I've got to try it on." Gwen modeled it for Harper.

"That hurts my eyes. How about this one?" Harper tried on a straw cowboy hat with the front and back brim bent downward.

Gwen giggled and shook her head. "It looks like someone sat on it."

"That means you're not trying too hard to look good. If you wear all new stuff, then people will know you're a beginner and haven't spent enough time on the horse to break in your clothes."

"Oh," Gwen said. She liked having her clothes look good. "I'd still dress it up."

"Like putting a peacock feather on it? Like a musketeer?"

Gwen laughed at the thought of a giant blue and purple feather sticking out of the hat.

"No, but I'd take off that black band and replace it with a bright-colored band."

"You're not very traditional, are you?"

"I like happy colors," Gwen said.

"I'm ready for some traditional vanilla ice cream."

The girls pushed their bikes to the ice-cream shop and each ordered a scoop to go. As they left the store, Olivia and another girl were on the sidewalk waiting to come inside.

When Gwen's eyes met Olivia's, she felt her face burn. "Hey, Olivia."

"Busy day, huh?" Olivia asked. She looked Gwen up and down and wrinkled her nose.

"Um," Gwen stammered. "It was . . . earlier . . . plans changed."

"Sure," Olivia said. She turned to the other girl. "Come on, you've got to try the ice cream. They make it from local cows. Better than anything you can get in Chicago." She walked into the ice-cream shop.

The other girl flipped her hair and followed Olivia.

"What's their problem?" Harper said.

Gwen turned and walked down the sidewalk. Her ice cream started to melt into a soupy mess in her paper bowl. Her stomach lurched.

"I think the heat's getting to me," Gwen said. "I need to go home."

She threw her ice cream in a trash container on the sidewalk, grabbed her bike, and started pedaling home.

Harper biked next to Gwen, but kept her balance

by just pedaling. Instead of holding the handlebars, she held—and ate—her ice cream.

At Gwen's house, Harper said goodbye. "Tomorrow we ride the horses to the dig. Remember to ask your mom about that bottle."

Gwen waved and then went in and flopped on her bed.

Olivia had seen her hanging out with Harper. She was going to think Gwen was lying and hiding stuff from her. She'd be right.

Gwen had been keeping her friendship with Harper a secret so she could keep her other friendships. Now she'd been busted. Whatever friendship she'd had with Olivia was probably over. And if Olivia rejected her, the other girls would too.

Gwen clutched her stomach as it did a somersault. She just realized . . . she was friends with Harper.

FIELD NOTES

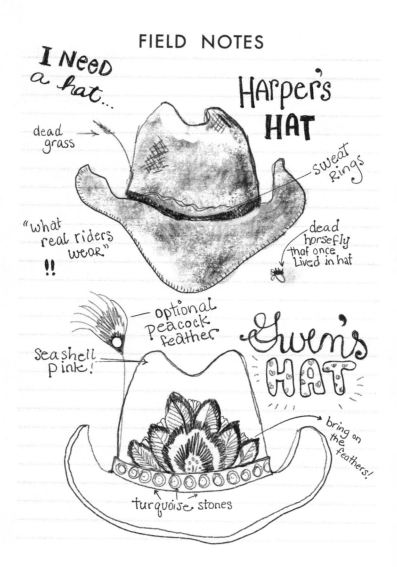

CHAPTER SEVENTEEN

"This is the only place I know you'll really be." Olivia had cornered Gwen at the end of marching band practice on Tuesday. "Can you hang out this afternoon?"

Gwen sighed. "I already have plans."

"With Harper?"

Gwen nodded. "How about tonight?"

"Got plans." Olivia emphasized the second word.

"With . . . who was that girl? Erin? Why haven't you told me about her?"

"Yes, with Erin," Olivia said, crossing her arms. "Because you're always too busy. Since when did you and Harper start being friends?"

"Last week. I've been helping Harper with a project—family history and archeology—and she's been teaching me how to ride a horse."

Olivia's eyes widened. "You? On a horse? I can't believe you even get close to them!"

"I'm getting use to them," Gwen said. "Except for cleaning up the manure in the stable. That reeks!"

"What does shoveling horse poo have to do with riding a horse?" Olivia said. "Are you sure Harper's not taking advantage of you?"

Gwen thought a moment. What she was doing for Harper was a lot harder than what Harper was doing for her. But Gwen had been the one who asked for Harper's help. And Harper had helped her.

"Actually, Harper's a pretty good teacher," Gwen said.

"Why do you want to ride horses so bad that you're choosing that over hanging out with me?"

"Di invited me to her family's trail ride for a week-long campout."

"Di, again," Olivia said, sighing. "More roughing it, huh?"

"I guess." Gwen shrugged.

"Sleeping on the ground, in a tent, and pooing behind a tree doesn't sound like fun to me," Olivia said.

Gwen twisted her bracelet. She hadn't thought about the lack of toilets. What do campers do without bathrooms? Even at the dig they had showers, toilets, and porta-potties. And if they slept in tents, how did they keep out snakes and mountain lions?

"Friends always tell each other the truth," Olivia said. "I do want you to meet Erin. I'll ask if I can bring you with me on Saturday."

"Thanks." Gwen smiled. Olivia was making peace with her. Maybe she was also okay with her friendship with Harper. "Would you see if Harper could come too?"

Olivia frowned. "I don't know. Harper might not feel comfortable."

"Why not?"

"What would we talk about? What if she came wearing her horsey clothes?"

Gwen twisted her bracelet.

"Honestly," Olivia continued. "You need to up your game too. You're starting to look like you've never seen the inside of a store."

"I haven't had time," Gwen said. "And my mom's been busy, too, getting ready for classes to start. We haven't even bought my school supplies yet."

"What's Harper's excuse?" Olivia said. "She dresses like a farm hand."

Gwen put her hands on her hips and narrowed her eyes. "What's wrong with farm hands? They're just as good as lawyers and the kids of lawyers.

Besides, clothes aren't the most important things in the world."

"Who are you and what have you done with Fashionista Gwen?"

"I'm still me," Gwen's voice rose. "It's just that there are other things I like too."

"At least start middle school looking like you belong to the twenty-first century. And do something with your new friend, too, or you'll end up sharing your unique fashion sense with only her."

Gwen studied her sneakers as she thought this over. Olivia was actually saying she and the other girls wouldn't be her friends if she dressed like Harper.

"Um . . ." Gwen had no answer.

She heard a gasp and looked behind her.

Harper stood there with her arms crossed, scowling. "Would that be so bad to be stuck with me?" She turned and stomped away.

Olivia looked at Gwen and raised an eyebrow. "Wow. Over-dramatic much?"

Gwen glared at Olivia. "Oh, grow up and quit judging people by their clothes!" She ran after Harper. "Harper, wait!"

But Harper jumped into her dad's truck and slammed the door. As the truck pulled away, Gwen saw Harper's face in the side mirror. Tears were streaming down her cheeks.

Olivia had acted like a jerk.

Gwen had been worse for not standing up for her other friend right away.

—

That afternoon, Gwen sat on her bed and texted Harper. "I'm sorry. I did stick up for you—after you left."

Gwen pressed send. Her message sounded so lame. She waited to see if Harper would respond. Then Gwen tried calling. No answer.

Either Harper had left her phone somewhere and was out with the horses, or she was ignoring Gwen.

That served Gwen right. Gwen had betrayed their friendship.

Friendship? Until the day before, Gwen had only thought of Harper as someone who could teach her something she needed to know. But Harper wouldn't fit in with Gwen's other friends. She didn't care about clothes and who wasn't talking to whom. She only liked her horses and books. She said what she thought.

Gwen admired that. Harper was confident and did what she wanted even if no one did it with her.

However, it wouldn't hurt Harper to think first

before talking. Gwen had felt more than one cut from Harper's sharp words.

All this drama was messing up their plans. Since Harper wasn't answering her phone, Gwen figured their riding and digging were off for the day. Now she would only have three more riding lessons before her parents' deadline. *If* she made up with Harper.

Gwen paced. She tried to play her flute, but couldn't focus on her music. She made a list of things she'd need for the trail ride. She paced again.

A whole day wasted.

She might as well go to the library and read more old newspapers. At least she could keep looking for clues. She texted her mom her plans, grabbed her notebook, and headed out the door.

—

After supper, Gwen's mom took her shopping for school clothes. When they arrived at the mall, Olivia and Erin and a handful of other girls were sitting on the benches near the main entrance, sipping smoothies, and laughing. Gwen tried to steer her mom away from them toward a side entrance. Her mom didn't get the hint and walked right up to the girls.

Gwen followed slowly.

The girls laughed at something Erin said.

"This girl thought she looked so great," Erin continued, "but Mom said she looked like she dressed herself from the sales rack." She giggled, and the girls copied her.

Olivia looked up at Gwen. She wasn't laughing. Olivia loved to shop from the sales racks.

"Hello, Olivia. Girls." Gwen's mom looked around the group and smiled. "I haven't seen you since early June. How was your summer?"

"Fine," Olivia mumbled.

Gwen twisted her bracelet. The girls must've come from Erin's private shopping party. She stuck out her chin. Who cares? She was still mad at Olivia, anyway.

"I see you've all been doing some school shopping too," Gwen's mom said, gesturing to the bags sitting near the girls' feet. The bags all sported the name of the mall's newest store. "We're just starting. Where should we go for the good deals?"

The girls glanced at each other and then stared at the sidewalk.

"Since you all like the same store," her mom said, "I guess that's where we'll start." She looked around the circle again, stopping at Erin. "I haven't met you before. I'm Gwen's mom, Dr. Bell."

Erin gave her a blank stare in return.

"Oh, you haven't met Gwen yet." She nudged Gwen forward.

Gwen's face burned. She wished she could disappear.

Erin then smiled at them like they were long-lost friends and extended her hand to Gwen's mom. "I'm Erin, and my mom manages the best store in the mall."

"Ah." Gwen's mom shook her hand and smiled. "Tell your mom you're an excellent marketing person. Well, we're off. Stop by sometime, ladies." Then she turned and headed to the mall's newest store.

Gwen hurried to follow but peeked back at Olivia and caught her staring at Gwen. Olivia quickly turned and began to laugh with the other girls. But Gwen also noticed Olivia's bag was a lot smaller than the other girls' bags.

"That was awkward," Gwen's mom said when Gwen joined her. "Erin pours the charm on a little thick, doesn't she?"

"That was embarrassing! I'm not five!"

"I'm sorry. I forget sometimes." Her mom reached out and touched her arm. "I haven't heard you talk about Olivia at all lately. What's up?"

"Nothing," Gwen said, shaking her head.

"Right," her mom said, drawing out the word.

"I think Olivia would rather be friends with Erin." Gwen swallowed the lump in her throat. "Besides, I'm too busy right now to do what Olivia wants to do."

"Your projects with Harper?"

"Yes, if Harper wants to keep working with me."

Her mom tipped her head and started to say something.

Gwen hurried on so she didn't have to explain. "I found a clue at the library that should get Harper really excited."

Her mom took that hint and changed the subject. "Now it's you and me time." She put her arm around Gwen's shoulder. "I didn't even bring my laptop. Let's do your shopping. Maybe you could even help me find a new first-day-of-school outfit."

Gwen smiled at her mom. This was a much different trip to the mall than the one they had done right before the field school dig when her mom was working on her laptop while Gwen was trying on clothes.

They went into the store that Erin's mom managed. It was all trendy teen clothes. Gwen pulled a cute t-shirt off the rack and held it up in admiration. Then she looked at the price tag. She nearly dropped the shirt. No wonder Olivia had a tiny bag. The cost of this shirt alone would've taken a chunk of Olivia's babysitting money.

Her mom checked the price and whistled. "Let's hit our regular store."

Gwen gulped and nodded.

What I need for CAMPING:

1. Toilet Paper
2. Hand sanitizer
3. Dry Shampoo
4. ~~Deoderunt~~ Deodorant
5. •Tick repellent
6. Lip Balm
7. Sunscreen

WHERE'S MY TOILET PAPER?

CHAPTER EIGHTEEN

Gwen almost ran to marching band practice the next day. She had to talk with Harper to clear the air from yesterday and to share her new clue before practice started. She paced on the sidewalk by the drop-off location. Harper wouldn't be able to avoid her and get to practice.

As Harper's dad's truck pulled up to the curb, Gwen bounced on her toes.

Harper got out of the truck and shut the door. She slowly walked up to Gwen. "I'm still mad at you."

"I deserve it," Gwen said. "I really am sorry."

"Yeah, seven texts gave me that idea. Listen, we don't have to be friends, but if you'll still help me, I'll help you."

Gwen figured that was as close to forgiveness as she was going to get. "Deal." She pulled out some papers from her backpack. "I went to the library yesterday, and I found something!"

"I found something yesterday too," Harper said. "I have to go get my cymbals, so save it for later. Can you come out to the farm today?"

Gwen nodded. "Mom said she could drive us over after practice and pick me up before supper."

—

At the farm, Harper led the way through the tack room to a door that Gwen had barely noticed before.

"What's this? A closet?" Gwen said, peering at the old equipment laying on shelving and scattered about. She peered into the shadows, wiping cobwebs off her arms.

"It's just an old storage room." Harper glanced sideways at her. "No one ever comes here except for me when I want to be alone." Harper pulled out two pairs of gloves and handed one set to Gwen. "I found this old trunk that has a bunch of family history in it."

"What are the gloves for?"

"Mice have been in the trunk."

"Eww." Gwen wrinkled her nose and took a step back.

"I don't do mice either," Harper said, "but there

aren't any in there now, just things they've chewed and pooped on. Hold your breath."

As Harper opened the trunk, Gwen got a whiff of ammonia from the mouse droppings. She gagged, then held her breath and peeked into the chest. There were a couple blackened trophies, something that looked like it might have been a saddle blanket at one time, and a metal box.

Harper pulled out the box. "Let's take this into the tack room."

Gwen nodded and hurried back through the door, taking a deep breath of merely stable air and horse odors.

Harper set the box on top of Gwen's bucket and opened it, revealing a stack of yellowed photos and letters.

The girls studied each item. One photo featured people in old-fashioned clothing, horses, and polo players standing in an open field near a river. The date written at the bottom of the photo was 1892.

"Here's the best clue!" Harper handed a letter to Gwen.

Gwen's hand shook a little as she read aloud:

March 1881, Miller's Valley, Yankton, Dakota Territory
My dearest Mary and children,

I've found our home and the beginnings of our new estate, which I have named Miller's Valley. It's humble now, but we already have a house, a barn, and a well. I'll soon acquire more livestock and plant our first crop.

I'm in awe of our Heavenly Father's gracious providence. Our family's new fortune will make us independent of my brother's whims.

Please forgive me for this late response to your letter dated last fall. The Dakota Territory has been in the midst of an exceptional winter, and snow has blocked the trains and the mail. However, our neighbors assure me that the climate here is quite conducive to raising a hardy family and the amount of snowfall this winter is exceedingly rare.

Make haste with your arrangements to come to me at the Yankton train depot. Bring King Alfred. Dakotaians love a good race, and our stallion will help us start a proper English-American bloodline.

Your loving husband and father,

B. Miller

The girls were silent for a minute.

"That's how my family knew about a fortune—my treasure," Harper said.

"I found out more about Basil's family too." Gwen pulled out the papers from her backpack. "I jumped ahead a few years in the newspaper to see what happened to the family and found this article. I made a photocopy so you could see it." Gwen handed it to Harper. "It mentions polo matches, teams from other places, and a really big match at Miller's Valley where a Miller was the leader of the local polo club."

The girls stared at each other.

"That match must have been on this farm," Gwen said.

"But we still don't know what the treasure was or where it is." Harper sighed and put the letter and the photocopy into the box.

"Now you know Basil's family and your family have more in common than relatives and a piece of land," Gwen argued. "You're also connected by a love for horses and polo. And you know that Basil's family made it through hard times. Knowing your family history is a kind of treasure."

"But not the kind of treasure I need," Harper said.

FIELD NOTES

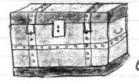 What we found in an old trunk...

 stacks of <u>OLD</u> Letters -- one from "Basil Miller"!

REALLY COOL <u>OLD</u> PHOTOS

  and mouse droppings. ~ew!!~

CHAPTER NINETEEN

A short time later, the girls had saddled both horses. Harper had put a western saddle on Boots, along with a set of saddlebags. The girls had packed their notebooks, phones, hats, and water bottles in Gwen's backpack and the small spade and trowel in the saddlebags, leaving the bucket behind.

They walked the horses into the arena and checked the cinch straps.

Gwen mounted Ruby.

"Ready?" Harper asked.

Gwen nodded, trying to make herself believe it. It felt dangerous to go where there was no fence to stop Ruby from running away with her.

Harper opened the gate, allowing Gwen to ride Ruby out of the arena. Then Harper mounted Boots, and as they came through the gateway, she leaned down, picked up the spade she had placed there earlier, and held it against her right shoulder just as she had held her polo mallet.

"Follow us, about a horse-length behind," Harper said. "This is what trail riding is like — slow. We're not racing or roping steers or playing polo." Harper clucked to Boots and nudged her with her heels, guiding her down the hill.

Gwen patted Ruby's neck. "Let's do this, Ruby." She nudged her into moving, and the horse plodded behind Boots and Harper.

They walked the horses the whole way. Gwen was stiff at first, but as Ruby ambled along, Gwen saw Ruby wasn't going to run off with her, and she breathed easier. She focused on relaxing her hips and back, and on moving with Ruby's movements.

After a while, Gwen looked around her. Their path out to the 1920s house was familiar by now, but Gwen was getting a different perspective from being on Ruby's back versus walking along the edge of the fields.

She could actually see over the top of the corn stalks. The ground sloped and the dark greens of the trees by the James River extended in a curvy line far to both the left and right.

Wispy clouds streaked the horizon, and the still, humid air quivered in heat waves. Flies buzzed around Ruby's eyes, and she shook her head and swished her tail.

Gwen's jeans protected her from the flies and from the saddle, but the denim felt heavy and absorbed the heat from the sunshine. Sweat rolled down her back. She pulled her shirt away from her skin and wished for a breeze.

Her helmet allowed some airflow, but with no breeze it mostly just trapped the hot air, and the chin strap chafed against her sweaty neck.

When they reached the 1920s house, Harper tied both horses to some sturdy lilac branches.

"Ugh. Riding the horses down here was hotter than walking." Gwen removed her helmet and sighed in relief.

"But it was more fun," Harper said. "And you rode Ruby!"

"I did, didn't I?" Gwen smiled.

The girls spent the next several hours digging in the hole where they'd found the bottle and where Gwen had put flags. They unearthed a metal spoon, an old-fashioned key, and pieces of what looked like a white plate.

But no treasure.

Harper took a drink of water and shook her empty bottle. "Time to quit for the day."

"I can't wait for a shower." Gwen stretched her

back, guzzled from her water bottle, and packed the artifacts in her backpack. She handed the small tools to Harper to pack in the saddlebags. Gwen picked up the riding helmet. She wished she didn't have to wear it, but she put it on.

She peered up at Ruby's back and wondered how she'd get up there. She looked around and saw a fallen tree. She led Ruby to it, stood on the tree trunk, and reached the stirrup.

Harper mounted from the ground.

"I'm going to have to learn how to do that," Gwen said as they headed back up the hill.

Harper turned around in the saddle. "Do you think any of those artifacts will give us any clues?"

"No." Gwen shook her head. "I think they're just interesting pieces of trash."

Harper frowned, turned forward, and was silent for a long time.

Gwen ran her finger between her chin and the chin strap to relieve the chafing. Why did she have to wear this? Ruby was walking very slowly. There wasn't any danger. She unsnapped the chin strap. That felt so much better!

She watched Harper's back. Harper seemed to think they were going to find a bag of gold nuggets, but she wouldn't say why she wanted to find it so badly.

Gwen doubted there was a treasure. She looked at the stalks of corn, unmoving in the breezeless heat. Perhaps Basil had meant the land itself was the treasure.

Gwen noticed Harper and Boots were a long way ahead of them.

"Harper," Gwen shouted. Harper didn't seem to hear her.

Gwen nudged Ruby with her heels and clucked to the horse, but Ruby barely increased her pace. So Gwen clucked loudly and dug her heels into Ruby's sides.

Ruby began to trot.

Gwen bounced in the saddle. "This—is—too—fast!" She dropped the reins and clutched the saddle horn with both hands.

As she and Ruby started to pass Harper, Gwen turned, shifting her weight. Her left foot slid out of the stirrup. Then a horsefly bit her on the back of the neck.

"Ouch!" Gwen swatted at the fly and bounced out of the saddle. She hit the ground backpack first, and her helmet went flying. She couldn't breathe. She lay on her back staring up at the clouds.

Suddenly Harper's face blocked her vision. "Wait 'til you catch your breath," Harper said.

Ruby stuck her muzzle in Gwen's face and

snorted, shocking Gwen with a blast of her hot breath.

Gwen gasped for air.

"Where's your helmet?" Harper demanded. "Did you hit your head?"

Gwen shook her head slowly. "The backpack."

"You're lucky," Harper said, scowling. "You could've gotten a concussion—or died."

Gwen closed her eyes and tears ran down the sides of her face.

"You should go to the doctor so you can get checked out, just in case." Harper stood and offered her hand to Gwen.

Gwen wiped her tears and let Harper pull her to her feet.

Harper then handed Gwen the helmet and studied her as she fastened it securely to her head. "I don't think you've broken anything, or you'd be in more pain. I've fallen off lots. Don't let a fall mess with your mind. I'll help you back on." Harper leaned over, ready to boost Gwen onto Ruby's back.

Gwen looked up at Ruby and remembered the helplessness she felt as she had fallen.

"No!" She gulped back a sob, turned, and walked toward the farmhouse.

—

That evening when Gwen and her mom came home from the doctor's office, Gwen walked stiffly into her house. "I don't care that I didn't get hurt. I'm never riding again."

"That's good to know now before I drive you all the way to Colorado," her mom said. "You know, if you don't ride, you won't get to see Di."

Gwen swallowed. "I know. But I wouldn't be good enough in two days for you to say I can go anyway."

Her mom squeezed her shoulder. "You'll see Di again. I feel sure of that. But you might regret not trying to ride again. Someday you may wish you hadn't let your fear make your decisions for you."

"I'll just stick with playing my flute and marching in band. I don't need any more excitement than that."

"Then you need to let Di know. She can either cancel your horse reservation or ask someone else to go in your place."

Gwen nodded. She knew she needed to tell Di, but she just couldn't tonight. She'd wait until tomorrow after she got home from Harper's. Even if she wasn't doing riding lessons, she should still help Harper look for the treasure.

That reminded her of the artifacts in her backpack.

"Mom, would you look at our artifacts? Can you tell me if they're valuable?"

Her mom looked at the pieces of broken plate. They were in smaller pieces now since Gwen had landed on top of them.

"These feel like china, but the lettering on the backside has worn off." Then she inspected the broken bottle. She cleaned it a bit better with a wet toothbrush and stared at the pattern in the glass, running her finger over the spiral ridges at the top.

"Interesting." She handed it back to Gwen.

"Well?" Gwen said. "How old is it?"

"I'm going to let you figure it out." Her mom pulled a thick book off her bookcase and plopped it into Gwen's hands. "You'll find it in here."

Gwen looked at the cover. It was a guide for nineteenth- and twentieth-century glassware. She flipped through some of the pages. There must've been thousands of photos of jars, bottles, plates, bowls, cups, and drinking glasses! She sighed. "At least give me a hint to know where to start."

"The color and these ridges at the top are the important parts."

"I already knew that," Gwen muttered. She lugged the book to the kitchen table and spent the next hour searching for a similar container in the guidebook. She read that jars and bottles with spiral ridges were machine-made during the twentieth century.

She looked through a section featuring Depression

glass from the 1930s and found a green saltshaker that looked just like her container.

Since the girls dug it up near the Millers' 1920s house, it wasn't old enough to be from Basil's family in the 1880s.

She and Harper were back to square one.

Depression Glass:

- ★ cheap glassware.
- ★ made in America by lots of companies.
- ★ popular during the GREAT DEPRESSION in the 1930s.

- ★ often made in different 'COLORS'.

CHAPTER TWENTY

Harper's mom drove Harper and Gwen out to the farm after band camp on Thursday morning. The two girls, along with Harper's brother and sisters, helped carry grocery bags into the house.

"Thank you," Harper's mom said as she gently lowered herself into a kitchen chair, put her feet up on another one, and rubbed the sides of her belly. "This little guy must want to be in marching band too. His feet haven't stopped moving since I picked you two up."

"How do you know?" Gwen asked.

"Would you like to feel? It's okay." Mrs. Miller waved her over. She took Gwen's outstretched hand and guided it to her belly. "Just wait."

Gwen wasn't sure what she was waiting for. Suddenly the side of Mrs. Miller's belly bulged, receded, and bulged again. Gwen squealed and then laughed. "That's so cool!"

Harper grinned. "It's really funny when he gets the hiccups."

"You can feel that?" Gwen said, widening her eyes.

Harper nodded.

Mrs. Miller heaved herself out of the chair. "I'll put the groceries away. You two make lunches for the littles and yourselves. Will you be okay on your own this afternoon? I'm taking the kids to Hayley's for a play date."

"Yeah," Harper said. "We'll be down at the old house."

Gwen twisted a bracelet and nodded.

After lunch, Gwen and Harper headed downhill.

"Let's ride the horses down to the dig again. It saves time to do your practicing on the way."

Gwen pulled her hat out of her backpack and plopped it on her head. "No. I'm done with horses. You can ride if you want, but I'm walking."

"What about the trail ride?"

Gwen swallowed. "Not going."

"Have it your way." Harper frowned. "But I'm not giving up an opportunity to ride. You can carry the big tools, and you might as well start walking."

Gwen headed down toward the river. Soon she

heard hoof beats behind her. She stopped and watched Harper ride the trotting Boots past her.

"I have bad news," Gwen said when she arrived at their dig. She pulled out the artifacts from her backpack. "This is a saltshaker, but it isn't any older than 1920. And the broken plate didn't have any clues for dates. Either we have a long way to go to dig deep enough to hit Basil's trash pit, or we're digging in the wrong place."

"Are you saying it's hopeless?" Harper said, putting her hands on her hips. "Or are you trying to find an excuse to quit since you don't want lessons anymore?"

"I'll stick to my part of the deal—at least until school starts." Gwen shook her head slowly. "I don't know of a better place to dig. I'm just saying don't count on us finding anything. Sometimes archeologists dig for years at the same place."

"I don't have years. Let's just keep looking. One of us digs in the trash pit, and the other one uses the metal detector between the trees."

Gwen agreed.

The girls spent the next couple hours detecting and digging. They found a few more burnt cans and broken glassware.

"The brush is so thick, it's hard to move the detector between the trees." Gwen rubbed her back where she'd landed on it the day before. "Let's stop for today. I'm really sore." She put the artifacts and her notebook in her backpack.

"We haven't been working very long. Just a little bit longer?"

Gwen shook her head. "Tomorrow."

Harper clenched her teeth. "Fine." Harper packed her phone and Gwen's tools back in Boots' saddlebags. She patted the horse and buried her face in Boots' neck. She sniffled.

Was Harper crying? What was the big deal to take the rest of the afternoon off? Gwen's Friday deadline didn't exist anymore. They still had five more days to dig before school started.

Harper mounted Boots. She held out her hand to Gwen. "Do you want a ride up the hill?"

"Behind you?"

"Where else?" Harper narrowed her watery eyes at Gwen.

Gwen shook her head and took a step back.

Harper snorted in disgust. She wheeled Boots around and trotted her up the hill.

—

When Gwen finally made it up the hill twenty

minutes later, she found Harper in the tack room weeping as she put away Boots' bridle and saddle.

"I called my dad to come get me," Gwen said. "He'll be here soon. Tomorrow, we need to go back to the library for more research."

Harper wiped the tears from her cheeks and glared at Gwen. "I thought archeologists were all about digging, not library research! You're not being much help!"

Gwen stepped back, surprised. "I've told you, archeologists aren't treasure hunters. I don't think there is any treasure. Basil just told a good story to get his family to move out here."

"Take that back!" Harper nearly spit out her words. "You don't want to keep your promise to me. Some friend you are! I've only got a few days—"

"A few days for what?"

Harper clenched her fists, brushed past Gwen, and raced through the doorway around to the back of the barn.

The magma from Gwen's inner volcano was bubbling. She ran after Harper and grabbed her elbow, squeezing hard.

"Friends? You said we didn't have to be friends. We made a deal. That's all. Now I won't be able to go to the trail ride to see my only friend before she goes away. It's your fault if I never see her again!"

"You wouldn't have lasted at a trail ride anyway." Harper's eyes flashed. She pushed Gwen's hand away. "You can't stand the horses, the flies, the smell, and you wouldn't get to wear your fancy clothes."

Gwen crossed her arms. "You wouldn't know what it was like to not smell like horse!"

"Smelling like horse is a good thing. But you reek like a vile, despicable promise-breaker!" Tears streamed down Harper's red face. She shoved Gwen and ran past her.

Gwen tottered and fell into fresh manure droppings.

Harper stopped and turned, hands clenched at her sides.

"We need money! The doctors think the baby has Down syndrome and will need special care. Mom quit her job. Dad took a second job to help with costs, but it's not enough. Now neither of them have time for polo or horses." Harper wiped her tears and took a deep breath.

"Saturday is our last polo match. Mom and Dad are going to list Boots and Ruby for sale. My baby brother is worth it. But the treasure could help my brother and maybe help me keep my horses. So see, soon I'll never smell like horse again!"

Harper's sobs shook her. She ran off, leaving Gwen sitting in manure.

FIELD NOTES

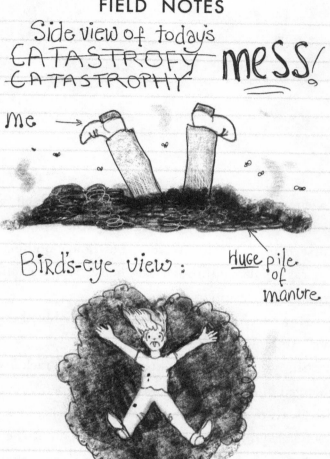

Side view of today's ~~CATASTROFY~~ ~~CATASTROPHY~~ **mess!**

Me →

Bird's-eye view:

Huge pile of manure

I will **never** smell good again.

CHAPTER TWENTY-ONE

Gwen picked herself up and sprayed herself with water from the hose, washing away the worst of the horse manure off her clothes, but doing nothing for the rage pulsing through her body. Her own inner volcano was erupting.

How could Harper do such a horrible thing to her? And then just leave her there?

She grabbed her backpack from the tack room, changed into her hiking boots, and stomped down the driveway, dripping the whole way. She wasn't waiting for her ride. She'd walk all the way home if she had to. And she was never going to talk to Harper again.

She was about halfway home, as water droplets rolled down the inside of her jeans into her boots causing her wet socks to chafe her feet, when her dad drove up next to her. She jumped in the car.

"Want to talk about it?" her dad said.

"No," Gwen said. She shivered as the air conditioning chilled her wet skin.

Harper was wrong. Gwen wasn't a promise-breaker. Gwen was just trying to be reasonable. Harper was never reasonable. She always thought she was right.

Why did Gwen ever think she and Harper could be friends? She let Harper come between her and Olivia and her other school friends. Maybe it wasn't too late to patch things up with Olivia.

Her dad opened all the windows and turned the car around toward home.

Gwen pulled out her phone and texted Olivia. "Want to come over?"

"Who's this?" Olivia texted.

Gwen bit her lip. She deserved the snark from Olivia. "You were right about Harper. Can we talk?"

"I'm going to the pool with Erin and some other girls. Want to come?"

"Yes!"

"What changed your mind?"

"I saw Harper's mean side," Gwen texted. "I'll tell you all about it at the pool."

Gwen's dad okayed Gwen's plans. "I have a meeting at school in an hour." He looked at her sideways. "After you shower I can drop you off at the pool on my way, and then you can walk home when you're done."

When Gwen got home she hosed herself off again, took an extra long shower, and threw her stained and rank clothing into the washing machine.

—

Later, at the pool, Gwen looked around until she saw Olivia, Erin, and the girls huddled around a few deck chairs.

Olivia waved her over.

Gwen put her worn, dirty backpack down next to Olivia's straw bag. "Hi, Olivia," she said. "Hi, Erin."

Erin stared at Gwen's bag, wet hair, and t-shirt and shorts Gwen was wearing over her swimsuit, and she scrunched her nose.

"Hey." Then she walked to the concession stand.

Olivia sighed and pointed at her straw bag. "What do you think?"

"It looks old."

"It's not old. It's vintage, and it's a designer brand. My grandma sent it to me."

"Okay . . ." Gwen wondered where this conversation was going.

Olivia leaned closer and whispered, "Erin said it

made me look—and smell—like an old lady. Everyone laughed."

"Don't pay any attention to them. You have more style in your pinky than they do. Let's go swimming."

"I don't feel like it." Olivia shook her head. "Go ahead."

Gwen wanted to forget Harper and Erin. She jumped into the water. As she came up, she savored the sun on her cool, wet skin. Now it felt good to be wet. As she shook the water out of her ears, she heard Erin's voice. "What's that smell?"

Gwen looked up.

"What smell?" Olivia said.

"I don't know, but it's coming from over there." Erin pointed at Olivia's and Gwen's bags. "It's worse than old-lady odor."

Olivia's lip trembled as she covered the bags with her towel.

Gwen's magma started boiling again. She pulled herself out of the pool and marched over to the girls. She dried herself with her towel right in front of Erin, standing close enough to make sure she dripped water on her feet.

"I come to the pool to have fun with my friends and to swim, not to sit around, look pretty, criticize others, and—" Gwen suddenly realized that at the beginning of summer—before the dig, before meeting

Di, Clay, and Cooper—that's exactly what she and Olivia used to do. She inwardly cringed.

"Some people are *so* sensitive," Erin said. She moved over to the next deck chair and scooted aside the girl already sitting there.

As Gwen put her clothes on over her swimsuit she faced the fact that she was a lot like Erin—or at least she had been. But since the dig she had thought she was so much more grown up than the other girls— especially Olivia. Now she was revolted by her own meanness and pride. For the second time in one day, Gwen couldn't wait to retreat home.

"I'm leaving," Gwen said to Olivia. "Want to come to my house?"

Olivia wiped her cheek and glanced at Erin.

"You don't have to put up with that." Gwen tipped her head toward Erin. "Friends don't treat friends like that."

"Thanks." Olivia shook her head slightly. "I'll stick around for a while."

Gwen grabbed her bag and walked home. It really was going to be a long school year.

—

Back home, Gwen sat on her bed, clutching a stuffed animal and thinking of her drama-filled day.

She promised herself she wouldn't put up with Erin's insults, even if it meant the other girls wouldn't have anything to do with her. Even if Olivia chose to be friends with Erin instead of with her. Gwen and Olivia's friendship might be over.

Her friendship with Harper was definitely over. But they'd had some fun together. They had laughed at some of the same things, and they had taught each other about things they each liked.

Had. Had. Had.

Gwen buried her face in her pillow. None of her friendships were working in the now. Now. Now.

Except with Di.

Di got her. She even liked Gwen when Gwen had lied to and stole from her at the dig. Now she wouldn't see her for years. At least Gwen could text and video chat with her for a few more weeks.

Now was a good time to do that. Besides, she needed to let Di know that she wasn't coming to the trail ride.

"Can you talk?" Gwen texted.

"Sure." Di texted back. "Just packing some things so one of my sisters can have my room. Do you want to video chat?"

"I'll call you." Gwen opened her laptop and sent the video chat request to Di who answered immediately.

"Hi, Gwen! I'm excited about seeing you in a couple weeks."

"About that," Gwen said, frowning. "I'm not coming."

"Because of school?"

"No." Gwen twisted a strand of wet hair around a finger until it hurt. "I didn't tell you before. I wasn't just taking lessons to learn how to ride, but because I'm afraid of horses. I thought I could get over it."

"But . . ."

"The lessons didn't work." Gwen paused. "Well, I did learn a little and thought I got past being scared, but then I fell off. I know you're supposed to get back on the horse right away when that happens. But I just can't."

"Are you hurt?" Di gave her a concerned look.

Gwen shook her head. "Just scared."

"It's okay," Di said. "I'm glad you tried. That took courage. But I'll miss you."

"I'm really sad not to be able to see you, especially —" Gwen's voice broke.

"Are you really all right?"

Gwen tried to say yes, but her voice wouldn't work. Instead, a tear escaped and slid down her cheek.

"Gwen, what happened?"

"I'm lonely. Olivia and I keep arguing. She thought I liked Harper, the girl teaching me how to ride, better than her. I think she likes her new neighbor, Erin, better than me. Erin thinks she's better than everybody. But I won't let her push me around. Plus, Harper and I had a huge fight. She even shoved me into a pile of horse poo! She's been mean before, but this was the worst!"

"Why did she do that?"

"She was mad at me for not helping her find her family treasure." Gwen thought a bit. "Di, when we were at the dig, I did some pretty bad things—even to you. Why did you forgive me and stay friends with me?"

Di sat back and put her finger to her lips before answering. "I've messed up, too, and others have forgiven me. I guess because I know what it's like to be forgiven, then I could give it to you."

"Harper said her parents need to sell the horses." Gwen twisted her hair tighter. "She loves all her animals. Especially her horse, Boots. That's why she was trying to find the treasure."

"She must be devastated."

"Their crops aren't good. And her newest little brother is going to need extra care. Harper wanted to help her brother, but she also wanted to try to keep her horses." Gwen took a big breath. "I was so mad at her. But she didn't do anything worse to me than I did to you. She was just super upset."

"Being upset doesn't give anyone a pass for treating others badly," Di said, frowning and shaking her head, "but if we see and understand what the person's going through, it may make it easier to forgive. It can still take a long time to trust again. And sometimes we need to stay away from that person for our own protection."

"How do you know if you should avoid the other person?"

"When you apologized to me, I could tell you really meant it. You weren't trying to manipulate me. I'd spent enough time with you to know that you were normally a good friend and that you were just going through a tough time."

"Thanks for being my friend." Gwen released the hair she'd been twisting.

Gwen and Di said goodbye, and Gwen closed her laptop. She pulled her knees up to her chin and wrapped her arms around her legs.

Di had offered friendship to Gwen at the beginning of the dig and didn't care if she was popular or fashionable. She didn't treat Gwen like a little kid, either.

Gwen had never offered friendship to Harper. She

had made a deal with her. She had used her. They had used each other.

Then Gwen and Harper had unexpectedly become friends. Gwen had trusted her with her fear of horses. Harper had shared her best friends, Ruby and Boots, with her. Gwen didn't feel like she had to be anyone other than herself with Harper, and Harper had even seemed to let down her guard with Gwen.

But Gwen hadn't really cared about why Harper wanted to find the treasure.

What about Olivia? They'd been friends a long time. They also knew and kept each other's secrets. Olivia had started off being mad at her because Gwen had been too busy talking about the dig and Di to care about what Olivia cared about.

Gwen had thought she'd grown up so much this summer, but maybe not as much as she thought. She really hadn't been that good of a friend to Olivia. She had treated both Olivia and Harper as if she expected them to be friends with her, but also like she was doing them a favor by being their friend.

Olivia had been right. Gwen could be a better friend.

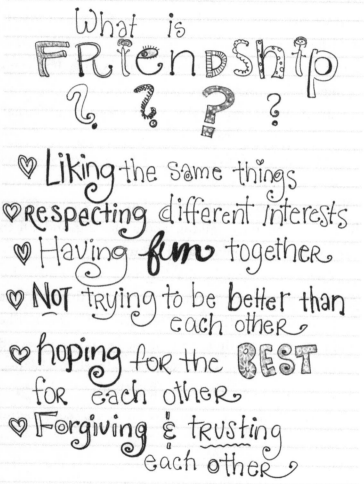

What is
FRiENDShip
? ? ? ?

- ♡ Liking the same things
- ♡ Respecting different interests
- ♡ Having fun together
- ♡ NOT trying to be better than each other
- ♡ hoping for the BEST for each other
- ♡ Forgiving & trusting each other

CHAPTER TWENTY-TWO

Gwen could start with a little understanding and forgiveness. She would offer Olivia and Harper friendship. True friendship.

What about Erin?

Gwen pondered this one. Olivia seemed to like Erin. Yet Erin treated Olivia terribly. In fact, every time Gwen had seen Erin, the girl was treating someone badly. She decided she would just keep watching Erin.

Gwen texted Olivia. "I've been a terrible friend for the past couple weeks. I haven't paid any attention to what you wanted to do. I see why you've been mad at me."

"Thanks for noticing."

"I'm really sorry. Will you forgive me?" Gwen

twisted her bracelet while she waited for Olivia to respond.

"I'll think about it. So what terrible thing did Harper do to you? You never told me."

"We had a fight about the project I'm helping her with. But now I understand why she wanted my help."

"More than just doing her barn chores?"

Gwen read the sarcasm in Olivia's text. "Yes. Her parents are going to sell her horses." She explained all about Harper's brother, the family treasure, and their dig.

"Are you still going to be her friend?"

"If she'll let me." Gwen thought a minute. "You know, we can have more than one friend. I still want to be friends with you—even if you are friends with Erin. Give Harper a chance. She has a polo match on Saturday. Come watch."

"I'll think about it."

Gwen sighed, texted bye, and then texted Harper.

When Harper didn't respond, Gwen tried calling.

There was no answer.

Harper was probably ignoring her like the last time. But this apology couldn't wait until band camp. Gwen could ride her bike to Harper's farm and apologize in person. It was going to be light out for hours, and it was only a few miles to Harper's house. She could ride there, make things right with Harper, and ride back before dark.

She texted her mom to get permission, grabbed her backpack and bike helmet, and headed to Harper's.

—

Gwen parked her bike next to the house. She looked at the sky in the west. The sun peeked between the gathering clouds, and heat lightning flashed. The air felt still and oppressive, like it was waiting for a coming storm.

She went to the front door. Harper's dog slept in the shade of the porch. He lifted his head, noticed Gwen, and went back to sleep. She knocked on the door and listened for movement inside the house. Nothing. The only thing she could hear was the buzzing of the dog-day cicadas.

Gwen walked down toward the stable. Boots stood outside the pasture fence opposite the half-empty stock tank. She was wearing her saddle and bridle. A broken lilac branch was caught on the dangling reins.

"Hi, Boots," Gwen said, skirting wide around the big horse. "Thirsty? Looks like you could use some fresh water." She unrolled the hose, dropped the nozzle into the tank, and turned on the faucet. Then she opened the gate and Boots walked right up to the water. "There you go."

Ruby strolled up to the tank from where she'd been nibbling grass.

Gwen held out her hand to the horse. "Hi, Ruby," she said, as the horse sniffed her palm. "Have you missed me? I actually miss you, but there is no way I'm ever riding you. Aren't you happy to be done with such a klutz?"

Ruby stretched her neck to sniff at Gwen's hair. Then she shook her head.

"Sad? Me too." She stroked the horse's velvety nose. "This is goodbye, anyway. You'll be going to a new home soon. I don't know how Harper's going to handle it." She looked around. "Where is Harper?"

Gwen left the pasture, turned off the water, and searched the stable. She peeked into the stalls, the outer tack room, and Harper's hiding place in the storage room.

No Harper.

Gwen pulled out her phone and called Harper's number. She heard the distant sound of a phone ringing. She walked toward the sound, close to the pasture. The phone stopped ringing, and Gwen dialed again.

The ringing came from Boots.

Not from Boots. From Boots' saddlebag.

Gwen's stomach tightened.

Harper wouldn't just leave Boots outside the pasture, saddled, and separated from the water.

Gwen went into the pasture and slowly walked to the horse. "Boots, where's Harper?" She reached out her palm toward the horse. She'd never touched Boots before. The horse was taller than Ruby.

Boots smelled Gwen's hand and then shook her head.

Gwen grabbed the reins and untangled the lilac branch.

Something was wrong. Harper was missing.

Gwen held out her palm to Boots again. As the horse smelled her palm Gwen reached out to pat her neck.

"Boots, we don't have time to become friends. I need to get Harper's phone out of the saddlebag, okay, so don't step on me. Please." She kept talking to Boots as she slid her hand along the horse's side to the saddlebag. Empty. Gwen went back around the front of the horse to the other saddlebag.

She pulled out Harper's phone. She checked it and saw Harper had not opened any of her texts or calls.

Something was terribly wrong.

"Where's Harper?" Gwen studied Boots' face as if

the horse would answer her. "Why's her phone in the saddlebag? Where are my tools?"

The lightning flashed in the distance. The air felt electrical.

"Harper went to our dig, didn't she?" Gwen asked Boots. "Did you run off and leave her there?" She told herself Harper was probably walking back to the barn and was probably hot and mad that Boots had left her. But her stomach tightened into a knot. Harper might have fallen off Boots—or something else might have happened to her.

Gwen stared at Harper's phone. "Should I call one of her parents?"

It felt wrong to look through her contact list, like she was invading Harper's personal space. Besides, she didn't want to make Harper's parents panic if Harper really was fine.

She'd check out the dig before calling the Millers. But walking down there would take a long time. She gulped. She should ride Ruby. But she didn't think she could saddle her on her own. Boots was already saddled.

A chill ran through Gwen's body and her arm hair stood on end. She shivered.

Boots was huge! Harper had said Boots was "too much horse" for Gwen, and she was right. Even Ruby was too much horse for her.

But if Harper was in trouble, Gwen needed to find her fast.

She reached out her hand to stroke the horse's nose again. Her stomach did a somersault.

"Cowgirl up," Gwen told herself. "Be brave." Gwen gulped and ran into the tack room where she donned a helmet and the old cowboy boots. She put both her and Harper's phones in her backpack.

Back in the pasture, she grabbed Boots' reins and led her out to the arena. She set the step stool next to the horse, but when she looked up at the horse's back, she began to shake. She wrapped her arms over her stomach and clenched her eyes shut.

"Harper would say to act calm, and then Boots will be calm." Gwen took a deep breath and opened her eyes. She stroked the side of Boots' muzzle and talked to the horse.

Boots flicked her ears toward Gwen as she listened.

"Okay, I'm acting calm and confident. I can do this."

Gwen climbed the step stool, held the reins against the top of Boots' neck with one hand and the saddle with her other hand.

Then she glanced at the ground and pictured herself falling off Ruby the day before and how hard the ground had been when she'd landed. She backed down off the stool and held her shaking knees.

"I can't," she said as she started panting in shallow breaths. "I'm—afraid." Then she remembered Di saying she didn't want to live her life in fear, and her mom saying that someday Gwen might wish she hadn't let fear make her decisions for her.

"Harper needs me." Gwen straightened and squared her shoulders. "I won't let fear run my life. I will do this."

Gwen quickly climbed the step stool and mounted Boots before she could chicken out again. She lifted her chin, sat tall, and pushed her heels down in the stirrup.

"Let's find Harper." Then she nudged Boots forward and pulled the reins to turn the horse toward the 1920s house and their dig.

Gwen focused on relaxing and moving her body to match Boots' gait. As she grew less frightened, she peered down the hill in search of Harper. She nudged Boots to go as fast as Gwen could take it without bouncing in the saddle.

Finally, she arrived at their dig. It was as empty as the house and barn.

"Boots, where's Harper? I thought you'd lead me to her."

The horse nibbled some grass under the lilac

bushes. One of the lilac branches was broken. That must've been where Boots had been tied up earlier.

Gwen slid off the horse and took off her helmet. She left it on the ground and tied Boots to the bush.

"Don't wander off without me, okay?"

Gwen checked out the trash pit. She could see some fresh digging, and she found Harper's water bottle and riding helmet. But no trowel and no Harper.

"Harper!" Gwen yelled. Nothing. She yelled again and again.

She strained to listen but only heard cicadas. Then she heard a faint "Help!"

"Harper? Where are you?"

"Help!"

"Keep yelling so I can find you!"

"Gwen!"

Gwen concentrated. It sounded like Harper was calling from up the river. "I'm coming! Keep yelling!" Gwen hurried along the edge of the trees looking for a trail through them. The woods were thick with brush. Finally she found a deer trail that went into the woods. "Harper! Where are you?"

"Help!" Harper's voice sounded closer.

Gwen plunged into the woods and followed the trail through the trees. When she reached the river-bank, she yelled again.

"Gwen," Harper yelled. "Over here."

Gwen followed the voice upstream around a bend and found Harper on her back wedged under a fallen tree on a slope next to the river.

"Harper!" Gwen rushed over to the girl.

Harper was covered in loose dirt, and the tree had her pinned across one shoulder and down the left side of her body. Harper's face was streaked with dirt and tears.

"I'll try to lift it, and you slide out."

"No," Harper cried. "Every time I move it shifts and gets heavier."

"I'll call for help!" Gwen dumped her backpack and found her phone. "Wait, how do I tell someone to find us? Where are we?"

"Call my dad," Harper said. "Tell him we're at the river near the picnic sandbar."

Gwen looked at the phone. No signal. She grabbed Harper's phone and checked. No signal. Gwen wanted to scream. "I need to go back up to the field to get a signal."

"Don't leave me!"

"Harper, I have to!" Gwen sat next to Harper. She handed her a water bottle. "Here's some water. As soon as I get a signal, I'll call and come back. Promise."

Harper nodded, tears slipping down her face.

Gwen took Harper's phone and scrambled back up the bank. She tripped over some weeds and fell, dropping the phone. "No, no!" She felt around under some of the leaves and found it. Then she hurried through the woods until she got back to the field.

She had a faint signal, so she opened Harper's contact list and dialed Harper's dad.

Nothing.

Gwen walked closer to the old house as she kept dialing. Finally, the call connected and Harper's dad answered. Gwen quickly told him what happened and where they were.

When Gwen ended the call, she glanced once more at Harper's contact list. It only had three names: Dad, Mom, and Dakota Digger. Gwen smiled. That was her.

She hurried back to Harper.

FIELD NOTES

When you can't draw hooves, draw grass!

CHAPTER TWENTY-THREE

"How did you get here anyway?" Gwen said as she sat with Harper in the shadows of the trees.

"I had to keep looking for the treasure." Harper looked away from Gwen. "But you were right. I don't think there's a treasure there — or anywhere."

"I'm sorry."

Harper turned back to Gwen and nodded. "Digging wasn't doing any good, so I just started walking. I didn't really know where I was going, just along the trees. Then I started following the trail all the way to the river. It was cooler in the shade, and I could hear water. It felt peaceful. I just kept walking." She wiped her teary face with her free hand.

"Then I got down here, and I saw the sandbar that we picnicked at when I was little. The sandbar's smaller than it used to be."

Gwen noticed Harper's feet were bare. "Where are your boots?"

"I don't know. Over there somewhere." Harper's voice trailed off and she closed her eyes.

Gwen glanced around and saw Harper's boots and socks by the edge of the water near a tiny sandbar. She turned back to Harper and shook her free arm. "Hey, stay awake. How'd you get under a tree?"

"I was soaking my feet in the water, and I saw something shiny." Harper opened her eyes. "It was sticking out of the bank, and I climbed up to check it out. It's metal, so it's from a person. Right?"

Gwen nodded.

"I still had your trowel with me, so I started digging around it. But the soil came loose and everything slid on top of me."

Gwen looked on the other side of the tree and noticed all the loose dirt.

"I think this tree came from the top of the bank." Gwen looked closer at the river bank. "I see part of a circle that looks like the gears on our bikes. It must be from a huge machine. Something bigger than a car."

"How'd you find me?"

"Boots."

"What?"

"You didn't answer my calls or texts, so I came

out. Boots was at the pasture, and your phone was in one of the saddlebags."

"I should've had my phone in my pocket, not the saddlebag."

"I was afraid you might be in trouble at our dig, so I rode her down here."

"You rode Boots?"

Gwen nodded.

"Way to go," Harper murmured. "Poor Boots. She must've thought I'd left her and decided to go home."

"Harper, Gwen!" Harper's dad's voice came from the woods.

"Over here," Gwen hollered.

Then everything happened fast. Harper's dad rushed down to them, followed by a couple first responders carrying a stretcher and some medical bags.

"I'm okay, Dad," Harper said. "I'm just pinned."

"Be still. We'll get you out." Harper's dad positioned himself near Harper's side and grabbed her jeans and shirt. The other two guys stood at each end of the tree, counted to three, and lifted the tree and inch or so, straining their arms and turning red-faced.

It was just enough that Harper's dad pulled Harper to the side and freed her. The men lowered the tree and held their breath waiting to see if the rest of the bank would stay stable. When the soil didn't shift, they exhaled.

One of the first responders checked Harper's eyes with a little flashlight, then he felt her head and neck and shoulders.

"Ow!" Harper began crying again.

"They'll do x-rays at the hospital," the first responder said. "But that collar bone could be broken. We'll take her back on the stretcher just in case there are other injuries."

The three men lifted Harper onto the stretcher and hauled her up the bank. Gwen grabbed the girls' belongings and followed. When they got back to the 1920s house, Gwen noticed the clouds had dissipated, and a cool breeze freshened the air.

The first responders slid Harper into the back end of Mr. Miller's truck and jumped in beside her. Mr. Miller slid into the driver's seat and looked back at Gwen. "Boots?"

She nodded. "I'll take care of her."

"Give her an extra good brushing," Harper called from the back of truck. "Then you need to do something with yourself. You look like a mess and smell like horse."

Gwen stood on the truck's back bumper and grinned at Harper. "You should see what you look like. And thanks. That's the nicest thing you've said to me. Are you delirious?"

"Thanks, friend," Harper grinned in return.

After the truck left, Gwen walked over to Boo and untied her. "Will you let me ride you back?"

Gwen guided the horse to the fallen tree, which she stood on to get into Boots' saddle. She and Boots returned to the stable as her parents' car pulled into the driveway.

As Gwen unsaddled and brushed Boots and turned her out in the pasture, she told her parents everything that had happened that day. By the time they stuck her bike in the trunk of the car to head home, the setting sun streaked orange and pink through the dark blue horizon.

Gwen yawned. She climbed into the back seat and closed her eyes. "I hope Harper's okay," she murmured before she fell asleep.

—

On Friday afternoon Gwen and her parents drove out to the Miller farm. Her mom went inside the house to help Mrs. Miller prepare supper that the two families were going to have together.

Gwen, her dad, and Mr. Miller rode in Mr. Miller's truck down to the 1920s house where Gwen

_sh_ the men what she and Harper had been
_d_ They walked down to the river and studied the
_ct_ Harper had discovered before her accident.

Then they came back up to the house and Gwen
went to Harper's bedroom where Harper was resting.
Harper was sitting on her bed, her left arm in a sling,
listening to Bea read a book aloud.

Gwen entered quietly and sat on the floor and
looked around Harper's room. It was her first time
seeing it. The room had two beds and a dresser and
mirror between the beds. A bookshelf filled with
books sat on the other side of the room.

Gwen looked at the titles of the books. Many were
horse books, like *The Black Stallion*, *War Horse*, and *The
Horse and His Boy*. A shiny silver trophy sat on the top
of the bookshelf next to a photo of Harper and her
parents and horses.

When Bea finished the chapter, Harper gave her a
hug. "Thanks for taking good care of me. Gwen can
take over now."

When Bea left, Gwen sat on the corner of Harper's bed. "How're you doing?"

"Fine." Harper sat up a little straighter and
grimaced as she changed positions.

"Honestly?"

"No," Harper said, eyes filling with tears. "I can't
play polo tomorrow. And I don't have any way to

keep the horses."

Gwen hung her head. "I wish we had found Basil's treasure."

"Me too. My dad told me that you were going to show him what I found. Was it any kind of treasure?"

"We just got back from the river." Gwen twisted the end of her braid around her finger and glanced around the room again.

"So not a treasure?" Harper said, sighing.

Gwen shook her head. "Dad thinks it's an old abandoned steamboat. It's not valuable."

"Rats," Harper said.

"Even if it was valuable, it wouldn't help you," Gwen said. "It turns out the river and river bank are public property, so the steamboat and any artifacts are too."

Harper slumped. "I wasted the last two weeks. I could've been riding Boots all this time." One tear slid down her face.

"I wasn't any help to you," Gwen said. "But you were a big help to me. My parents are going to let me go to the trail ride if you keep giving me lessons—for pay."

"Really?" Harper's face brightened. Then she frowned. "But we're selling Boots and Ruby."

"Your dad said they'd put off selling the horses for

a couple months and keep trying to find a way to keep them."

Harper gulped and nodded. "So it's just temporary?"

Gwen nodded.

Harper grinned. "It's better than nothing! Let's start lessons on Monday. You still have a lot to learn."

"I guess you won't be doing marching band anymore," Gwen said.

"Not the cymbals." Harper patted her sling. "But Mom talked to the director, and I'll be his assistant. I'll get to order you all around."

"No!" Gwen rolled her eyes. "You already do that at lessons!"

"So you're used to it," Harper said, laughing. "The first thing I want you to do is play the National Anthem at our polo match tomorrow."

"Truly? That'll be my first solo performance!"

"Is that a yes?" Harper said.

"Yes!"

"I have another surprise for you at the match."

"What?"

"Wait and see." Harper leaned back, closed her eyes, and smiled. "You know, at your lessons you're going to have to put on all the tack and do the grooming all by yourself since I've only got one good arm. You'll have to scoop all the manure too."

Harper's eyes popped open and she sat up. "The manure. I was so mean to you. I'm so sorry."

"Yeah, but I lived," Gwen said, shrugging. "I wish you had told me about your brother and selling the horses sooner. Friends are supposed to be honest with each other. But friends are supposed to be understanding. I'm sorry I was only thinking of myself."

"We'll both do better," Harper said.

Gwen smiled and nodded. She looked around Harper's room and thought about their new friendship and Harper's horses. Gwen was getting what she wanted—making a new friend and getting to see an old friend at the trail ride. But unless something major happened, Harper's family was still going to have to sell the horses. It would just be in a couple months instead of weeks. And Harper wouldn't get to play polo anymore.

Gwen looked up at the trophy on top of the bookshelf. "Is that trophy from playing polo?"

Harper nodded.

"It's fancy," Gwen said.

"It's a big deal to me that we won the championship," Harper said. "But the trophy is just plastic. In the old days trophies were made out of sterling silver."

"Silver?" Gwen's heartbeat quickened. "Like the trophies you found in the trunk?"

A slow smile spread over Harper's face.

Gwen jumped off the bed and helped Harper up. The girls ran out of the room.

"Dad," Gwen yelled. "We have something to show you! Now!"

FIELD NOTES

CHAPTER TWENTY-FOUR

Saturday morning, Gwen stood on the edge of a large grassy field at another farm outside of Yankton. She wore one of Harper's old blue polo shirts, a pair of blue jeans, and her new pair of cowboy boots she needed to break in before her trail ride.

Gwen turned as Harper, riding Boots, paraded around the field.

Harper used her right hand to hold the pole for the American flag while the end of the pole sat in a cup-like holder attached to her right stirrup strap. She held her reins in her left hand, but close to her body because her left arm was in a sling. However, Harper guided Boots mostly by using her legs.

Harper did know her horse stuff.

She and Boots were in their "uniforms." Harper wore a helmet, gloves, her blue team shirt, white breeches, and tall black boots. Boots wore wrappings on the lower parts of her legs, and her tail was braided and tied.

Also in uniform, Mr. Miller rode Ruby, whose mane was newly roached, just to the left of Boots and Harper.

The two horses walked all the way around the field and then to the center where they faced Gwen and the announcer holding a microphone.

Gwen's knees wobbled as the announcer introduced Gwen to the other players and the spectators. Then she brought her flute up to her mouth, took a deep breath, and began the first notes of *The Star-Spangled Banner*. She closed her eyes and visualized each note of the song she'd been working on all summer.

When she ended the song and opened her eyes, she grinned and the spectators cheered. A few months ago, she wouldn't have dreamed she'd do her first big solo performance at a polo match. Yet here she was.

After she put her flute away in her parents' car, Gwen joined Harper at the side of the field where she was standing and watching her team start the match. Mr. Miller was going to play, and he'd alternate riding Boots and Ruby.

"You hardly used the reins to guide Boots," Gwen said. "I'm impressed!"

"You should be." Harper laughed. "I told you I could."

"It was all Boots."

"It was *partially* Boots," Harper admitted, shrugging her shoulders. "And Dad. I really couldn't do much with the reins, so he stayed close in case Boots got spooked. Normally we'd trot around the field, but Dad said, 'Absolutely not.'" She deepened her voice to imitate her dad.

"I was impressed too," came a voice from behind them.

Gwen and Harper turned to see Olivia.

Gwen's jaw dropped. "You came!"

"I decided if you could stand up for yourself—and me—then I could too." Olivia smiled sheepishly.

Gwen beamed.

Olivia kicked at a clump of grass. "Someone told me we could have more than one friend, and I wanted to see what polo was all about." She turned to Harper and held out a bracelet that matched the ones she and Gwen wore. "I made this for you, if you want it."

Harper smiled and accepted the bracelet. "You were smart enough to wear boots. Want to hear what Gwen wore her first time around horses?" She looked sideways at Gwen.

"Not funny." Gwen playfully shoved Harper.

"Ow," Harper grimaced exaggeratedly.

Gwen started to apologize when Harper and Olivia laughed.

"Ha, ha," Gwen said, but she smiled on the inside. The three of them having fun together was something else she hadn't expected. "I like what you're wearing, but it's more rodeo than polo."

Olivia turned slowly around so Gwen and Harper could admire her button-up shirt, the silver-accented belt, and her western ankle boots. "It all came from the thrift store."

"That's where we shop!" Harper said. "But I'm not going to have time for a while."

"What else are you going to do with that arm in a sling?" Olivia said.

"My parents thought since I helped Gwen get over her fear of horses, that I—we—could teach anyone." Harper teased. "We're going to start a riding lesson business."

"Glad I could help." Gwen bent her knees and spread her arms in an exaggerated curtsy. Then she grinned. "Does that mean you're keeping Boots and Ruby permanently?"

"We'll see how the new business goes. The treasure is a big help too."

Olivia's eyes grew wide. "You found a treasure?"

"Not at our dig," Gwen said, bouncing on her toes.

"Harper found some antique polo trophies in a storage room."

"They're made of sterling silver!" Harper said.

"What about keeping your family history?" Olivia asked.

"We'll take photos of the trophies and give copies of all the articles and photographs to the town museum, but we've decided we'd rather have the horses than the trophies." Harper's eyes glistened.

Gwen smiled at Harper and Olivia. This was going to be a great school year.

Just then a group of players on ponies thundered by in pursuit of a small white ball.

"Go, Dad!" Harper cheered. "Go, Boots!"

Gwen admired the ponies and riders. Then she turned to Harper. "We don't have a clue what's happening. Start teaching!"

FIELD NOTES
BOOT GIRLS!

[my new boots!

friends!

AUTHOR'S NOTE

Yankton is a real town in South Dakota that lies near the James River and on the banks of the Missouri River. The winter of 1880–81 was known as the Hard Winter, and Yankton did suffer from devastating floods the spring of 1881 because of ice jams on the Missouri and the large amounts of melting snow. In fact, that flood destroyed many steamboats.

I've tried to honor Yankton's history while also creating fictional characters and places, such as Miller's Valley, Gwen's parents' university, and various stores. All the characters in this story, including Harper and her ancestors, are fictional, with one exception. Laura Ingalls Wilder was a famous author who wrote about her teen and young adult life in and near DeSmet, Dakota Territory.

The Press and Dakotaian was the name of the local

newspaper in the early 1880s, and it still exists, with a simplified spelling, as *The Yankton Daily Press and Dakotan*.

Yes, there is polo in South Dakota. The sport came along with English immigrants in the late 1800s to the area where Minnesota, Iowa, and South Dakota meet.

Although I haven't found that there was ever a polo club connected to Yankton itself, I do know that English immigrants brought the sport of cricket to the town, so it's possible that there was also a polo club somewhere near Yankton at some point.

However, there is currently a polo club in Sioux Falls, South Dakota, and one of the club members is my riding instructor.

Archeologists, like Gwen's parents, search for artifacts that give clues about the past. Sometimes they find things that are worth a lot of money—a treasure. But they often find items people have thrown away that aren't worth money. These artifacts are still a kind of treasure because they help us understand our history.

If you're interested in archeology, you might be able to join a club. Perhaps your state or a nearby university has a club that welcomes amateurs. Sometimes there are even opportunities for volunteers to help with digs.

Please never dig anywhere without permission from your parents. Many states have laws that require you to call a special telephone hotline before you do any kind of digging—whether for archeology, fences, trees, or gardens—to request utility companies mark any buried wires or pipes. Safety first!

Author Oscar Wilde once said that life imitates art, and that has been true for me during the creation of *Boots and Buckets*.

I had spent more than a year researching and writing this book, and all the major events and themes were complete. Then during the editing process, at one of my lessons, I fell off a horse.

When I got my breath back I realized I needed to get right back on that horse because if I waited I might become too frightened to try again. I knew I couldn't in good conscience talk about Gwen facing her fears if I couldn't do the same thing. So I remounted and continued my lesson!

Then a few weeks later I had another bout with fear that I couldn't overcome on my own. I developed a major case of anxiety (unrelated to horses). With help from God, prayer, friends, a counselor, a doctor, and medication, I'm working on not letting fear rule my life.

If you have a fear that is controlling you and making you miserable, I encourage you to talk with a parent or a teacher. Sometimes asking for help is a huge step forward in overcoming our fears.

Be brave,

Deb Watley

South Dakota, 2020

ACKNOWLEDGMENTS

Thank you to my editor Natalie Hanemann of Hanemann Editorial for helping me polish Gwen's story as if it were one of Harper's sterling silver trophies. Thank you to my illustrator Tiffany Harris for making Gwen's personality sparkle.

Thank you to my writing and reading buddies who have given me great feedback and encouragement on the creation of this book, notably Yettee Girard; Katie, Hayley, and Lily O'Connor; Bea Barker; and Katie Krueger for taking on the whole manuscript.

Thank you to Deb McGuire of Performance Plus Arabians, Sioux Falls, South Dakota, for the opportunities to take lessons and hang around "horse people." Thank you to Rebecca Barker, my riding instructor, for being much kinder than Harper and for encouraging me to ride through the scary stuff.

And finally, for answering my many questions and allowing me to participate at a field school, thank you to Dr. L. Adrien Hannus, professor of Anthropology, who also holds the David B. Jones Distinguished Chair in Anthropology and is the director of the Archeology Laboratory at Augustana University, Sioux Falls, South Dakota.

Any mistakes are mine.

ABOUT THE AUTHOR AND ILLUSTRATOR

Deb Watley lives in South Dakota where she loves to ride horses and read and write about archeology, history, horses, treasure hunts, and friendships. *Summer Ruins*, the first novel in the *Field Notes of Gwen Bell* series, earned a 2019 Oregon Christian Writers Cascade Award.

Sign up for Deb's email newsletter at www.DebWatleyBooks.com or connect with Deb at Instagram.com/DebWatleyBooks.

Tiffany Harris is a high school art instructor and an award-winning illustrator. She earned the 2016 Moonbeam Children's Book Silver Medal for *Freddie the Frog® and the Invisible Coquí* by Sharon Burch. When she's not teaching or drawing, Tiffany loves to zip around the farm on her yellow four-wheeler.

Visit www.tiffanytree.com to see more of Tiffany's artwork or connect with her at Instagram.com/tiffanytreeart.

CPSIA information can be obtained
at www.ICGtesting.com
Printed in the USA
FSHW011202031220
76410FS